THE
DOWAGER'S
WAGER

THE
DOWAGER'S
WAGER

•

Nikki Poppen

AVALON BOOKS
NEW YORK

Published by Thomas Bouregy & Co., Inc.
160 Madison Avenue, New York, NY 10016

Library of Congress Cataloging-in-Publication Data

Poppen, Nikki, 1967-
    Dowager's wager / Nikki Poppen.
        p. cm.
    ISBN 0-8034-9787-3 (hardcover : alk. paper)   1. London
(England)—Fiction.   2. Nobility—Fiction.   I. Title.

    PS3616.O657D69 2006
    813'.6—dc22

                                                2006003148

PRINTED IN THE UNITED STATES OF AMERICA
ON ACID-FREE PAPER
BY HADDON CRAFTSMEN, BLOOMSBURG, PENNSYLVANIA

For Grandma Ellen (1918–2003) who read romances with me avidly for years and wished me good luck in New York with my first manuscript four days before she left us for a better place. I love you!

For Mom (1942–2000): Thanks for typing my first manuscript when I was in fourth grade. You always believed. I wish you could see this.

For Bronwyn Nichole: You're my lucky charm, baby girl.

I want to thank my agent at Greyhaus Literary Agency, Scott Egan, for all his assistance. He has spent countless hours acting in the role of critiquer, agent and publicist on behalf of this manuscript. He was there with me every step of the way from helping me clean up the manuscript to make it publisher-ready, selecting the right publishing house for this story (Avalon was right on the money, the perfect place), skillfully guiding me through the process of seeing a book published to being a diligent publicist, going above and beyond the call of the agent's duty.

I want to acknowledge my Dad and his new wife, who married nearly forty years after going to their Senior Ball together. The story of their reunited first love sparked the idea for Isabella and Tristan's story.

Finally, thanks to my supportive P.E.O. chapter which has encouraged me every step of the way and always believed I could do this. I love all of you.

Chapter One

London, June 1809

If he had known what awaited him inside his town house, the young Viscount Gresham might have kept walking. As it was, he expected nothing, which increased his level of surprise exponentially. Unsuspecting of anything amiss, he opened the door to his town house and came to an abrupt halt one step inside the black and white tiled foyer. The tune he'd been whistling died on his lips and whatever hard won peace he'd achieved in the last few tumultuous weeks evaporated at the sight that lay before him. He hardly heard the door close behind him, shutting out the noise of the street. All of his attention was fixed upon the woman seated on the small settee set against the wall.

His guest did not hear him immediately, giving Gresham a moment to let her astonishing beauty wash over him. Each time he saw her it was like seeing her for the first time all over again. This afternoon, she sat erect, holding her posture as rigid as a model sitting for a painter. Quite a picture she made too, in the fine fabric of her deep blue muslin walking gown. A white chip bonnet dangled by its ribbons from her hand, leaving her face fully exposed. Her profile was as perfect as any Italian cameo and just as pale. Aware of his presence at last, she turned her head towards him. Upon seeing him, she rose swiftly and came to him, desperate words falling from her lips as she took his hands in her own.

"Marry me, Tristan. Only you can save me now," Isabella Hartsfield pleaded softly. Her topaz eyes glistened with real tears as she lifted her face to his.

How was he to resist this cry for help? Tristan speculated, gently disengaging her hands and setting her firmly away from him. With his whole heart he wanted nothing more than to grant her plea but his overly honorable conscience argued he must persevere. She was betrothed to another and set to marry in three days.

This was not the first time she'd pleaded with him to rescue her from this unwanted marriage to the upstanding but aging Marquis of Westbrooke. Her parents had arranged the match in order to restore the empty family coffers after the failure of two business ventures. He wondered if Isabella knew how dire her family's financial situation was.

Tristan turned away from her beseeching gaze so she could not see the depths of his own frustration and so he would not be tempted by the desperation in her own. "Isabella, you know we cannot wed. No one would receive us if we eloped. We'd be outcasts among our own people." The rationale sounded impotent on his lips, even to himself. If he did not believe it, how could he expect Isabella to see the need to do the honorable thing?

"Do you truly care about such things, Tristan?" Isabella came up behind him, boldly encircling his waist with her arms. She leaned a cheek against his back. "I never imagined you did." Her voice was not much above a whisper.

Tristan glanced around anxiously. They stood in full view of any servant. Such physical closeness would lead to disastrous rumors. Isabella was impulsive but she was not careless. Today, she was both—a telling testament to the level of her desperation. Tristan turned to face her, his movement breaking the circle of her arms. "Did anyone see you enter? You are courting scandal by coming here unchaperoned. It does not matter that I am your brother's best friend. This is still considered a bachelor residence and you are still a young lady."

Isabella's eyes sparked at the scolding. Tristan knew he'd made a misstep. He had hoped to provoke some penitence from her for such rash behavior. Instead, he'd made her angry. "Don't talk to me of propriety when you're the one stealing kisses on dark balconies. If you had minded your manners at Lady Soffitt's rout, I wouldn't find myself in this bumblebath."

"Give over, Isabella. That's not fair. You liked my kiss." Dash it all, conversing in the hall was deuced awkward. They could not stay here and have this discussion. Tristan was annoyed at himself for saying the first words that popped into his head. Decisively, he ushered Isabella into the privacy of his study and shut the doors firmly behind them.

"What are we doing in here?" Isabella asked, looking around the decidedly male domain of walnut paneling and leather.

"I am saving your reputation and that of your future husband's," Tristan retorted more sharply than he'd intended. He riffled a hand through his dark hair and apologized. This would be the last time he'd see her alone before she married. He didn't want to ruin it with angry words.

"At least now we can speak freely," Isabella said with an equal sharpness that reminded him not so much of the demure young woman who'd sat in his foyer, but the hoyden that lay beneath her feminine charm, the one who wore breeches and rode neck-for-nothing with her brothers and his friends. He loved them both.

"I don't understand your reluctance, Tristan. You told me you loved me on Lady Soffitt's balcony. It was the happiest moment of my life. Can you imagine what a sapskull I felt like when my father called me to his office and told me he had received an offer for my hand? I knew the offer was yours, Tristan. But yours wasn't the name my father spoke.

Instead, it was the marquis of Westbrooke, a man forty years my senior who I have only danced with three times in my two seasons." Isabella's voice quavered. Her eyes widened. "Did you even speak to my father? You're like a second son to him. If he knew, he would not refuse you." She reached for his hands again. This time he gave himself over to her touch.

"Your father knew. He refused. I spoke with him the morning after the Soffitt rout before Westbrooke visited." Tristan felt his stomach roil. He could not bear much more of the agony of letting her go.

"Why?" Isabella was all innocent disbelief. In that moment, Tristan knew she hadn't been told. It wasn't fair that he had to be the one to tell her. But it was less than fair that she not know.

Tristan took a deep breath and expelled it in a weary sigh. "I am twenty. I won't inherit my funds until my twenty-fifth birthday, five years away. Five long years in your father's reckoning. Your father needs money now. Whether you know it or not, your family is on the brink of financial ruin. A series of business ventures have gone badly and the losses must be recovered." It went unspoken between them that the marquis's overflowing coffers were the antidote to her family's ailment. "Your father made it plain to me that I must let you go for the sake of honor and your family." As yet, it was unclear to Tristan if he could be that strong when he loved her so much.

It would be the ultimate test of his character. His wild Gresham side, the side that had prompted his father to follow the Royal Marriage Act and restrict access to the family fortune until his twenty-fifth birthday, wanted to beg Isabella to run away with him. He would leave with her this minute. They'd walk out the door and down to the docks with nothing but the clothes they wore. They'd marry aboard a ship to the Americas. He would support them with nothing more to pawn than the ring on his finger and the strength of his back. He'd heard there was land for breeding horses in

Virginia, there for the taking. Isabella would love that. But Tristan said nothing, reining in his unlikely fairy tale. He was silent, letting her absorb the shattering news of the last few minutes.

The expression on Isabella's face indicated she understood perfectly what was required of them both. She had not known all the facets of the situation. Now that she did, she would do all that was necessary to protect her family. Tristan saw the instant in which her decision was made. The fire in her eyes that had burned so recently with the passion of her pleas to marry flickered and went out, leaving her beautiful face devoid of the liveliness Tristan loved. In its stead was a façade of calm serenity adopted by a woman who was resigned to her fate for the greater good. She released his hands. They were blanched in places where she had clenched them in disbelief at the story he'd told her.

When she spoke, her voice was stiff with formality. "I apologize for coming here. I understand now, how my being here today has placed you in an untenable position. I forced you to reveal things best left unsaid. I hope this will not reflect on your friendship with my brother. He loves you dearly. Again, I must beg your pardon for my rashness. I acted brazenly and only thought of myself." She made a hasty curtsy and exited the study, stopping to pick up a pelisse and reticule from the settee that Tristan hadn't noted earlier. He followed her out, wanting to offer some comfort, wanting to prolong the inevitable farewell. All the élan for which he was known failed him.

Her hand was on the knob of the door, the hall butler being either thankfully or discreetly absent from his post. Tristan called her back in a voice hoarse with anguish. "Isabella, a kiss before parting?"

Isabella halted. For a long moment she hesitated before turning to face him. When she did, he could see her throat working. He could see the struggle in her eyes as the flames briefly rekindled. He saw the sparks sputter and go out. He knew he'd lost her before she spoke. "I think that would not be prudent, my lord." The door opened and she moved beyond his reach forever.

He was left with one kiss. One kiss to weigh against a lifetime. Miserable and heartsick, Tristan slid down the wall of the foyer next to the potted palm and buried his head in his hands. The town house was infernally silent, except for the long case clock's loud ticking as it marked off the beginning of life without Isabella. He would have to leave England. He could not stay here and watch her become the wife of another. *The wife of another.* At the thought, his stomach churned. He grabbed for the basin of the potted palm and was violently ill.

It was generally held that all women were beautiful on their wedding day. Isabella Hartsfield hoped she would not be the exception. Not usually given to vanity, today she regarded herself critically in her bedroom's long pier glass. After much consideration, Isabella found herself to be in agreeably high looks, as long as one discounted the paleness of her face. No amount of cheek pinching could dismiss the porcelain whiteness that bordered on pallor. There was nothing she could do about it now. In less than an hour, she would be escorted by her father to St. Georges for her wedding to the fifty-eight-year-old Marquis of Westbrooke, Anacreon St. John. She had turned nineteen in May.

Isabella drew a deep breath and pressed her hands against her fluttering stomach as if she could still the churnings inside. Nervousness mixed with anxiety. She reminded herself sternly that she was a lucky girl to marry so well and so far above her position as a country baron's daughter. She was living the fairy tale of every young woman in England. Not only was she about to land herself in the lap of luxury, she was doing her duty to her family—a duty they desperately needed her to perform if they were to pull through their recent hard times.

A knock at her bedroom door commanded Isabella's

attention. She turned from the long mirror and smiled at the sight of her brother, Alain, poking his head around the door. Her smile widened when he shut the door behind him and let out an appreciative whistle. "Bella, you look lovely."

Alain came to stand behind her. They had always looked a great deal like twins in spite of the two year age difference between them. Both were tall and slender in build with the same honey-colored hair, the only difference being their eyes. Hers were tawny-colored. His were a sharp moss green that missed nothing.

"Is it too much, Alain?" Isabella asked, fingering the voluminous folds of her white silk skirt. "The modiste said the gown took twelve ells of fabric. Father could have re-roofed half the village for that." She gave a poor imitation of a laugh. Guilt tinged her voice. If she had felt guilty about the luxury of silk, she'd felt even more guilty about the hundreds of pearls used to trim the bodice. Her father was a comfortably wealthy baron by country standards and while she'd had plenty of dresses growing up and even London made fashions for her two seasons, she'd never worn a dress of such expensive magnitude. But the marquis had insisted.

The gown was an elaborate creation, reflecting the marquis's preference for the style of the previous century with its fuller skirts and tightly fitted bodices. Made from the finest of French silk, the wedding dress displayed his taste as well as his wealth. The material was an enormous extravagance due to the escalating war with France. These days, Portugal was the only remaining port still open to English merchants.

Alain tweaked one of her carefully arranged curls. "The dress is suitable for who you are now. Society would expect nothing less from the Toast of the Season and a future marchioness. Rumor at the clubs is that Westbrooke is head over heels for you and this dress shows it. Everyone will be angling to get a good look at you in it."

Isabella grimaced at the thought of a public display. "Growing up, I didn't imagine my wedding being such a public spectacle. It was to be a simple country affair in our little stone church, decorated with wild flowers and Vicar Hurley presiding." She could hear the panic rising in her voice. Alain must have heard it, too. He reached to clasp her hands in his.

"Bella, your hands are like ice. Are you all right? Come sit down."

Isabella laughed at the ridiculous notion. "In this dress? I don't think it is possible. Don't fuss. I'll be fine. I am just a bit jittery. Everyone expects so much from me today. I don't want to let them down." By everyone, she meant their parents and the marquis, who were all of the same age. They were good people even though she privately felt the three of them put too much stock in public appearances and opinion.

Alain nodded sagely. She knew he shared her opinion on the matter. Then he cleared his throat, a sign which Isabella had learned over the years signaled he had something difficult to say. She looked at her brother quizzically as he began.

"I think your room is the only peaceful place in the house. Everyone has gone mad with last minute preparations." Alain offered a tremulous smile at his joke before turning serious again. "But I didn't come up here simply to seek some peace. I also came up to thank you. I won't pretend that I don't know why you're doing this. Westbrooke is a good sort, but I know you wouldn't have chosen him on your own. I feel awful that you have to do this for me. If I could have found an heiress . . ." His voice dropped off in helplessness.

"It is a daughter's lot in life," Isabella said placidly, revealing none of her earlier thoughts on the subject. The less said the better. Speaking her mind or admitting painful truths would not change the course her life was taking. She had seen with her own eyes the pain her visit had caused Tristan. She would not inflict that same pain on her brother. Her brother needed this marriage.

"Nonetheless, I thank you." Alain smiled again and squeezed her hand. "Because of your brilliant match, Father will be saved from financial scandal and even ruin. The marquis will cover the debts and the new investments until they pay off." He smiled reassuringly. "Bella, St. John is a fine man. I believe you will find a measure of happiness with him. He'll treat you well and he's a refined gentleman with plenty of Town Bronze. He can establish you as a brilliant hostess or trendsetter if you wish it."

Alain paused before going on, seeming to debate internally with himself over some subject. "Bella, may I be so bold as to ask if there was someone else you preferred? I couldn't help but wonder when you were describing the wedding you'd thought you would have, who did you imagine the groom would be?"

Isabella looked at her brother queerly. Had he guessed where her heart lay? She hoped not. She would not have her brother bear the guilt of believing she'd given up true love for duty. She masked her shock with a playfully scolding tone. "La, Alain, have you been reading a Gothic? That sounds like something straight from a novel."

Alain shrugged his shoulders. "I have often wondered if there was someone else."

"I had only a season and a half before my engagement. I daresay there wasn't time to establish a tendre." Isabella smiled gamely, doing her best to put a damper on the conversation.

An awkward silence fell between them. Isabella struggled for something to say before she gave herself away under Alain's intense gaze. "Are Chatham and Giles downstairs? I thought I heard them earlier. They were hoping to come up before we left for the church."

Alain brightened at the mention of their childhood friends. "I'll get them." He added in a hushed tone, "I have it on good authority that Giles has some excellent smuggled champagne with him, as usual."

Isabella smiled. "Then by all means, send them up. We'll have just enough time for a toast."

Alain headed for the door but Isabella called him back.

"Wait, Alain. Is Tristan here?" She had to know. She needed a few moments to prepare herself for seeing him.

Alain turned slowly from the door, reaching inside his morning coat. He was somber when he spoke. "I didn't want to bring it up on such an auspicious day." He handed her a flat calling card. "He left this for me last night. Actually, a messenger brought it. I expect Tristan was gone before the note even arrived. Turn the card over."

Isabella carefully read the note written in Tristan's firm hand and looked up at Alain in disbelief. "He's joined the army. He's arranged for an officer's commission in the cavalry?"

Alain nodded. "He means to join the peninsular campaign in Spain."

The news hit her like a fist to the stomach. For a moment she couldn't breath. Her heart pounded as if it would hammer straight through the suffocating confines of her bodice. Since Napoleon's December seizure of Spain, the peninsula had seen heavy fighting. She'd overheard remarks at a recent rout that being sent to Spain was tantamount to suicide these days. Was that what Tristan was looking for? She held Alain's steady gaze as their shared fears for Tristan passed unspoken between them.

Alain did his best to allay her concerns. "Tristan can look after himself. I imagine he'll be back someday with a chest full of war decorations. I'll get Giles and Chatham."

What utter foolishness! What did a viscount's son know of soldiering? Isabella thought as Alain left the room. She wanted to sit down but couldn't, hampered as she was by her heavy skirts. Instead, she gripped a bedpost in an attempt to steady herself. What had possessed Tristan to suddenly join the army? Her Tristan was in the army, a lifestyle so at odds with who he was. He loved horses and roses. Yet he was gone. He had left without saying good-bye to his friends and it was her fault.

Isabella knew instinctively that his sudden departure had to do with her and she cursed herself for being twenty times a fool. She should have known he would do something like this. Two months ago, Tristan had withdrawn quietly to save everyone embarrassment once her engagement had been announced and his own suit had been rejected. But she had foolishly pressed him into an indelicate situation by speaking her feelings out loud. She had *begged* him to marry her. Her cheeks burned with remembrances, ironically bringing the much needed color to her face. Tristan had left to save her from future encounters with him, encounters that might discomfort them both.

Tristan had done the honorable thing by leaving but now she wished his gentleman's code to perdition. Honor and embarrassment were nothing compared to what Tristan risked in the army. She would not forgive herself if any harm befell him because she'd gone soft in the noodle and thrown herself at him.

By the time Alain returned with Chatham, Giles and the champagne, Isabella felt thoroughly miserable. She was certain she had sent Tristan to his doom through her outrageous behavior towards him. The champagne warmed her, although she was careful only to moderately sip it. It would be time to go soon and there would be more champagne toasts later. Already, she could hear the noise of the throng gathering along the sidewalks outside the town house to watch her progress to the church.

Laughingly, Giles and Chatham played at maids, helping her arrange the gossamer-thin veil over her hair. Alain gave her a brotherly kiss on the cheek and it was time. As she floated down the stairs in a white cloud of veiling and silk, Isabella wondered if it was the champagne or if all brides felt as if reality had become suspended.

Her father sat across from her in the open landau, her vast skirts taking up most of the space. Alain rode next to the gleaming black carriage on a white horse, periodically offering her encouragement while she smiled and waved to the crowd. As she rode to the church in her elegant equipage, arrayed in a dress that equaled the annual income of fifteen farmers, Isabella reminded herself that she was living a fairy tale. All she had to do was find a way to live happily ever after. She owed Tristan that much for all he'd given up on her behalf.

Chapter Two

London, February 13, 1816

The bitter February wind whipped at the hem of Tristan's caped greatcoat as he walked along prestigious Grosvenor Square with his companion and old schoolmate, Alain Hartsfield, the young Baron Wickham. Beside him, Alain leaned in close to his ear. "Let's go up and surprise Isabella," Alain suggested spontaneously. He veered towards an immaculate red brick, Georgian mansion on their left without waiting for Tristan's approval.

"Westbrooke left her the town house when he passed away two years ago," Alain commented offhandedly, pushing open the wrought iron gate leading to the front door with its fanlight pediment.

Tristan halted as the gate swung open, his pulse speeding at the prospect of seeing Isabella again. Alain hadn't mentioned anything about visiting Isabella this morning when Tristan agreed to lunch at Brooke's.

"Perhaps this is not the best time to call," Tristan hedged, suddenly hesitant. He hadn't planned on encountering her so soon after his return home, or for that matter, encountering any of his close acquaintances. It had been purely by accident that he'd run into Alain last night at the club. While he was more than glad to reconnect with his closest friend, Tristan wished the reunion could have been postponed. There was unfinished business he must see to before his military career would be officially over. It would be best to fulfill those obligations alone. Still, being reunited with Alain felt good—a true homecoming after a lonely sojourn.

Alain laughed and clapped Tristan on the back. "Don't be ridiculous. It's the perfect time to call and this is the perfect surprise for my sister. Isabella will never guess my surprise is you. It's been seven years. If it hadn't been for the military dispatches naming you occasionally, we'd all have given up hope of setting eyes on you again ages ago, Old Man. Can you imagine the look on her face?"

Tristan could indeed imagine Isabella's face. Her face had become his haven of sanity in the insane world of war. He had summoned it countless times in the past years when he needed to remember that true goodness yet existed in a world gone mad with blood, vengeance and greed for power.

As to the exact look her fair visage would wear upon hearing Alain's news, he did not care to speculate. He doubted the look on her face would be the look her brother was expecting. They had parted awkwardly, if not badly, seven years ago. In fact, their parting had been the impetus behind his abrupt decision to purchase an officer's commission in the army and go abroad.

Now he was back and she was a widow. He'd had a night to let the news penetrate his mind. Alain had mentioned Westbrooke's death at the club the prior evening, catching him off guard. In a perfect world, he might expect he and Isabella had another chance at love, but his world was far from perfect. *He* was far from perfect. His bad hand twitched inside his York tan glove in blatant reminder of the imperfections he'd acquired.

Nonetheless, he knew what he wanted. He wanted Isabella with a single-minded purpose that had sustained him throughout the war. Regardless of the countless odds against him, he had to try. If he could lay siege to the

fortresses of Spain, he could surely woo the heart of the love
of his youth.

"Are you ready?" Alain broke into Tristan's thoughts,
looking at him strangely as he rapped on the door with his
silver-headed walking stick.

Tristan cleared his throat, trying to dispel his anxiety.
"You should at least go up and prepare her first. I'll wait in
the foyer."

An expressionless butler opened the door and ushered
them inside. Alain looked at him once more in question.
Tristan shook his head and motioned him to go up with a
sweep of his hand. Alain shrugged, leaving Tristan in the
foyer alone with his racing thoughts.

The last time he had seen Isabella he'd been a different
man. At that time in his life, he prided himself on being a
man of honor; although in reality at the age of twenty, he'd
scarcely been a man. And he had not been honorable. He'd
kissed her even though Alain had hinted to him earlier that
same evening of a betrothal with the marquis. Then he'd run
like a coward. He'd run from the feelings she stirred in him,
and from his duty to her. Any gentleman knew better than to
kiss a young lady without making his intentions known, but
Tristan had stolen that kiss without declaring his feelings,
knowing that a declaration would be futile.

Certainly, he went through the form of addressing himself to her father, a man Tristan had known and admired for
much of his adolescence. But it had been a painful interview
for them both. Isabella's father was in no position to enter-
tain his request for Isabella's hand and it clearly upset him
to refuse Tristan, who he and his wife had succored in the
years following Tristan's parents' death.

Tristan paced the fashionable marble-veined foyer pretending to admire the collection of Dutch landscapes on display, meanwhile speculating on Isabella's reaction to his
return. Had she forgiven him for raising her hopes and then
dashing them? He'd wanted to sample her guileless love,
taste the lightness that she brought into his world. He'd

wanted to know what such innocence would feel like in his arms, to hold perfection within his grasp. He was on the verge of seeing in the flesh the vision which had sustained him through dark years on the Continent. Now that the moment was upon him, he both relished and feared it.

Isabella looked up from her letter writing in her private second floor parlor as the butler announced her brother. She smiled and rose to greet him with a kiss on the cheek. "Alain, I am so glad to see you," she enthused. "The weather has been too dismal for going out and I've grown bored with my own company. Sit down and tell me what you're doing out on such a bleak day."

She led him to a set of comfortable chintz-covered chairs framing a pale yellow sofa near the tasteful maroon-marbled fireplace, which put out an admirable amount of warmth to ward off the blustery day. Isabella's private parlor was eternal summer with its soft jonquil upholstered furnishings, cherry-colored draperies and pale yellow walls. She sat down on the sofa and motioned for Alain to join her.

When Alain didn't sit down, Isabella looked at him expectantly. "What is it?"

"Bella, I have brought you a surprise." His face beamed his excitement. He looked utterly boyish in his pleasure as he rocked back and forth on the balls of his feet.

Isabella laughed, finding her brother's enthusiasm contagious. "What is it?" She looked around curiously. Alain held nothing in his hands and no objects bulged suspiciously from his deep coat pockets.

"It's not a 'what'. It's a 'who'. He is downstairs. He wanted me to give you fair warning first." Alain's green eyes danced with merriment.

"Who? I can't possibly guess who is in town that I haven't already met." Isabella insisted, furrowing her brow as she racked her brain for an answer to Alain's riddle.

Alain delivered his *coup de grace* with great delight. "Since you'll never guess, I'll tell you. It's Tristan."

Isabella's smile faded and a hand went to her throat. "Tristan? He's downstairs?" Emotions rocketing through her, Isabella rose and walked to the window. She pulled back one of the draperies and made a great show of looking out the window while she struggled to marshal her rioting feelings.

She was definitely surprised. Years ago she'd convinced herself that he was gone for good. She would never see him again. As much as it had hurt to contemplate a life without Tristan, she'd learned a valuable lesson. Her girlish whimsies had nearly cost him his life. Such intense emotions were best kept under tight rein like her highly prized temperamental Arabians. In the ensuing years of his absence, she'd built a fortress around her heart that both sheltered and repaired it. She did not counsel herself to coldness; such a thing was not in her warm nature. However, she did counsel herself towards caution. She would not expose her heart so easily again. She heard Alain's easy voice in the background of her thoughts as he went on about Tristan's return.

"It is a wonderful surprise, isn't it? He surprised even me. The bounder didn't send word of his return to anyone. I ran into him by accident at Brooke's last evening. Isn't it splendid, Bella? It'll be like old times having us all together again. I've invited him to the Denbighs' Valentine masquerade tomorrow night." Alain's boots clicked on the floor as he strode to the door and spoke to the butler. "Regis, send up Viscount Gresham."

The words galvanized Isabella's thoughts. She smoothed the cranberry folds of her high-necked merino wool gown with sweat-slicked palms. She looked well enough in the dress but her heart raced at the prospect of being seen by him. What would he think? She hoped he would see her as a mature Society matron. She had grown up and was well beyond the silly girl who had irresponsibly doted on him and placed him in abject danger with her affections. Silently, Isabella vowed to make it up to him. Whatever he wanted or needed, she would provide. There must be something her old friend wanted that she could obtain; after all she was the widowed Marchioness Westbrooke with social standing and a fortune at her disposal.

In spite of her resolve, she trembled at the prospect of seeing him again. The past had been unleashed from the dungeon in which she had locked it. Nothing had shaken her carefully constructed fortress so much as the mere thought of Tristan waiting downstairs, not even her congenial husband's sudden death. A second set of boots sounded on the walnut hardwoods of her private parlor. It was time to prove that she was all that she thought she was—an adult woman past the first blush of infatuation. Her fortress was under siege.

Unable to put off the moment any longer, Isabella turned slowly to face her guest. "Viscount Gresham, this is an unexpected visit." Although her legs threatened to become jelly, she was gratified that neither her voice nor her eyes wavered when she met his penetrating gaze and looked upon the breathtaking whole of him.

Tristan had always been well formed and endowed with more than his share of good looks. Military duty merely served to enhance his virile appeal. It was impossible to ignore the broad width of his shoulders beneath the superbly tailored layers of his deep blue wool coat and pristine white linen. Neither could she ignore the muscular thighs encased in tight-fitting breeches nor the spotless Hessians that hid his well-shaped calves from further inspection. It was little wonder his reputation had grown apace during his years on the Continent. He had become a powerful-looking man. She was undeniably as drawn to him now as she had been in her youth, if not more so.

Her gaze traveled back to the sculpted planes of his face and the dark hair he wore defiantly long and tied back with satin ribbon. She noted there was a hardness to his features that had not been there before. A man had been chiseled from the boy she once knew. Isabella found the good grace to blush as Tristan gave her an imperceptible nod, acknowledging his awareness of her scrutiny.

"My Lady Westbrooke," Tristan stepped forward to take her hand and briefly skim it with his lips. Her pulse raced at the contact. She told herself it was because she rejoiced in her friend's safe return, but she doubted it had been wise to put herself in such close proximity. Her carefully constructed defenses shuddered under the attack.

Alain laughed. "Such formality! I assure you, it is not necessary between old friends in a private residence. I, for one, will not stand on such ceremony."

Isabella gave an awkward half laugh as she reclaimed her hand from Tristan's burning grasp. Thank goodness he wore gloves. "Of course, Alain is right. This stiffness is not needed. I shall ring for tea. Please be seated."

She busied herself with going to the bell pull, feeling Tristan's chocolate eyes surreptitiously following her about the room as he and Alain settled themselves in the chairs near the fire. His study made her feel self-conscious. Did he approve of what she'd become? Did he see that she'd done all that he'd asked of her that fateful day? Did she still stir him as she had of old? Goodness knew the mere sight of him in her parlor had all too easily roused her old passions.

Although Tristan had steeled himself as best he could downstairs, he had not been prepared for seeing Isabella. He had half hoped that Isabella would refuse to see him, all the while knowing that her sense of good manners and her loyalty to Alain would not permit her to do such a thing.

Tristan scoffed at himself as he watched her settle on the sofa. He'd only *thought* his memory of her had remained undiminished. Either it had dimmed considerably, or she had become far more beautiful with the passing of time. At the age of twenty, he'd regarded her as Copernicus did the sun, the golden center of the world's light. Then the light had gone out and his life had become dark. Today, the sun reentered his orbit. The honey-gold hair she shared with her brother was piled high on her head, spilling random ringlets to frame her face with its expressive topaz eyes, classic razor-straight nose and sensual mouth. The promise of her youth had been fulfilled in the goddess who sat to his left. She had become his Diana, with her height and athletic grace. Even though he had given her up in physical form, she ran through his blood and his spirit. He would never be truly parted from her, although God knew how hard he'd tried to sever the bond.

He drew his mind back to the conversation with a jolt, realizing how far afield he'd let his mind wander. Isabella was addressing a remark to him, her sensuous lips framing each word. "You must tell us all about your adventures in the army. Alain told me you were mentioned in the dispatches several times."

He winced slightly at the mention of the dispatches. What had the dispatches mentioned about his service to England? Surely they hadn't mentioned the form in which his service took place. For the sake of secrecy, the dispatches could not have mentioned anything beyond his services as a cavalry officer.

Turning to Alain, Tristan fell back on the distraction of humor. "Since when have you become interested in military affairs? The last I recall, horses held the sum of your meager attentions, my friend."

Alain answered the gentle ribbing pointedly. "Since my dearest friend joined the army without any notice. Perhaps someday you will tell me what provoked such rash action."

Tristan heard the latent hurt in Alain's voice. They had once been closer than brothers. He acknowledged Alain's concern with a short nod. "Someday," he concurred. Someday he would explain how he'd fallen in love with his friend's sister. Someday, he would explain how his military career was nothing more than a façade for rendering secret service to the crown. Someday. But not today or any time soon. Not while one final enemy lurked in the shadows of his life.

An awkward silence fell between the three of them. Isabella spoke up brightly. "The dispatches, Tristan," she said, grasping at the last topic of conversation before Alain's sensitive comment.

Tristan would have preferred any conversational offering but that. What to tell them? He couldn't begin by saying, "I hunted down men who were disloyal to the English cause and killed them." Neither could he begin with "I have come home because the last man I hunted got away and nearly killed me in his escape." With a casual smile at odds with his inner turmoil, he began to regale Isabella and Alain with a few harmless military stories while Isabella poured the newly arrived tea from a clever London styled rectangular teapot.

Tristan struggled to keep his train of thought on his tale as he watched Isabella's deft hands handle the tea service, skimming lightly from cream pitcher to sugar bowl. The simple acts were done with the same grace with which she did all things. He found it mesmerizing. He was struck with an urgency to reach out and grip those hands. A simple touch from her would complete his homecoming. Of course, doing so was impossible. Her brother was present and then there was the issue of his scarred hand. He wasn't ready to talk about that wound yet. Alain coughed and Tristan realized he'd stop talking in mid-sentence.

Hastily, Tristan regrouped, reaching out to take the cup from Isabella, careful to accept it with his right hand, his good hand. "Ah, I was just admiring the tea service. My apologies, I found them a bit distracting."

"The set is by Adam Buck. I attended one of his exhibitions and was quite taken by his design," Isabella supplied helpfully, pointing out the trademark round-bottomed cup featuring the mother and child motif associated with Buck's work.

Alain reached for his own cup and prompted Tristan. "You were telling us about Spain."

"Ah yes, the battle at Ciudad Rodrigo, but such tales are

best left for the club and the company of gentlemen." Tristan glibly dismissed the topic.

"You're home to stay, then? Truly?" Alain asked when it was evident Tristan could not be encouraged to share further.

"Most definitely, Alain. I have come home to devote myself full time to the care of my estates and the establishing of my nursery." Tristan cast a covert glance at Isabella to see how the announcement affected her. He was rewarded with a slight blush as she suddenly took an inordinate amount of interest in arranging the tea service.

"Are you really thinking of getting leg-shackled?" Alain's incredulity over the prospect was evident in his voice.

"Yes indeed. I hear marriage is necessary for setting up a nursery and begetting an heir in this part of the world." Tristan said dryly. "What about yourself? Should we do it together, old friend?" Now that Alain had inherited, he had to take the founding of a nursery seriously. Tristan was surprised Alain was yet unwed.

"Egad, man, we have a year yet until we're thirty. I am putting it off until the last minute. When I am thirty, I'll start looking seriously. I figure that will take about five years," Alain said in all sincerity. "Why are you so set on it? Do you have someone in mind?"

Absolutely Tristan thought. The only problem was that he was unsure of her heart. There could only be one wife for him and she would be Isabella. He had much to atone for, but he intended to win her forgiveness and her heart. He had come home expecting only to be able to worship Isabella from afar. It had been an unexpected boon to hear of Westbrooke's passing. Out loud, he said to Alain, "The military changes a man's outlook on his own mortality. I find that I prefer to wait no longer to ensure my future. Having been gone so long, I find I will need guidance when it comes to likely candidates. I hope to rely on you."

Alain laughed a bit too loudly. "I am not sure I would know much about wifely candidates. I avoid them like the plague, but I will offer you what advice I can." He nodded in his sister's direction. "Isabella would be the best mentor in this area. She's a bang-up hostess and knows everyone."

"That is a splendid idea, Alain," Tristan agreed. It was the perfect excuse for keeping Isabella close and claiming her attention during social events. He had told Alain the truth. He was home to stay and he did plan to marry soon—just as soon as Isabella would consent to it. He would need a bit of time.

Tristan inclined his head towards Isabella in an accepting gesture. "I will welcome your input about all the eligible young ladies." It was almost too much to tear his gaze away from her. He wanted nothing more than to drown in her presence. Trying to disguise his desperation, Tristan sent a querying look to Alain. He was relieved to see Alain set down his tea cup and rose to initiate taking leave. Tristan needed to clear his head of Isabella's intoxicating presence before he did anything rash that would put her off him for good.

Alain bent to kiss Isabella's cheek in farewell. "It's time we are off if we're to keep our luncheon appointment at Brooke's. I'll see you tomorrow night when I pick you up for Denbighs' party."

Tristan came forward and bowed over Isabella's hand. "Thank you for a delightful visit and for your assistance." He looked up from her hand to hold her gaze meaningfully. "I will look forward to renewing our friendship." He managed a lite pressing of her fingers, the merest of squeezes, to reinforce the authenticity of his words. It was not at all the kind of touch he envisioned earlier over the tea service, but it would have to suffice until a time when his touch could be otherwise. Was it his imagination or did her hand tremble slightly beneath his?

After she heard the front door shut and knew the gentlemen were truly gone, Isabella poured herself another cup of tea to soothe her jangled nerves. Heaven help her, Tristan was a fine figure of a man! Along with a handsome physique and chocolate eyes that could melt the hardest of hearts, the man imbued the essence of good manners.

That was the problem. His manners had been so impeccably perfect that she hadn't the slightest glimpse into the true nature of his heart. Did his good form hide his anger over her actions, which had cast him from the life he might have had and into his military exile? Or, were his good manners a sign that she was forgiven and that he might even look upon her with the fondness of an old friend?

The girl she'd once been would have bluntly asked him for the direct truth. The respected matron she'd become knew such a course of action was folly. Isabella took another sip of tea and counseled patience for herself. Carrying out her charge of finding Tristan a wife would give her ample opportunity to draw him out in conversation in order to discern his feelings for her.

Finding Tristan a wife brought another wave of conflicting emotions. On the one hand, she was delighted to be of use to him. It would be a way she could make the past up to him. She would find him a beautiful, wealthy bride with fortune and position so that the world would be laid at his feet. On the other hand, the thought of handing Tristan over to such a paragon of noble womanhood turned her stomach. Once he married, he would no longer be hers.

Isabella jumped up from the sofa, determined to squelch her selfish misgivings over the task. She crossed the room to a small Sheraton writing desk and took out pen and paper. She would start Tristan's wife search immediately by composing a list of the eligible girls who would be at the masquerade tomorrow. It would be fortuitous to begin on Valentine's Day.

Chapter Three

February 14, 1816

The Denbighs' masquerade proved to be an excellent venue for Tristan's return to Society. Leaning against a pillar in the respectably crowded ballroom, Tristan conceded that he could not have contrived a better event himself. Two attributes of the affair worked in his favor. First, the moderate population of people who attended the Winter Season abetted his need for a quiet re-entry. By nature, Tristan didn't think of himself as a highly social creature, reliant on the entertainments of London for his amusement. He favored the pace of life in the country, preferring the delights of his stables and greenhouse. Second, the masquerade by definition literally cloaked everyone in anonymity.

Wearing the required domino and mask, he could be both seen and unseen. It suited him perfectly. To promote mingling among anonymous guests and to help people determine the identity of their cloaked fellow party goers, the Denbighs had designed the affair based on the ancient Roman celebration of the pagan holiday. When guests arrived, the women wrote their names on a piece of paper and put the slips in an urn on the center table in the foyer. Once most of the guests had arrived, two footmen divided

the names between them and took them around to all the
male guests who would draw a lady's name from the vase.
The woman was to receive the man's attention for the entire
evening. He was to fulfill her every desire within reason.

Much tittering and laughter filled the ballroom as men
mingled through the crowd attempting to guess which
cloaked lady was the woman he'd drawn. There were sufficient amounts of people present so that the first hour of the
ball passed with people simply trying to find their partners.
Tristan thought the idea quite ingenious if not slightly scan-
dalous for those who wished something more daring. He'd
drawn the name of a Miss Caroline Danvers. He caught sight
of Isabella conversing with a small knot of people across the
ballroom. A wave of jealously swept through him when he
thought of another man dancing attendance on her. Next to
him, Alain swore softly.

"This is a devilish situation. I can't draw my sister's name
as a Valentine. I don't wish to be that *Roman*." He flicked the
unfolded paper in Tristan's direction revealing Isabella's
name.

The pagan gods were smiling on him tonight, Tristan
thought. "I'll trade with you, Old Chap. Isabella can introduce me to any Eligibles." He hoped he sounded casual as he
made his suggestion.

Alain looked at the name on Tristan's slip. "That's grand.
I know Caroline. She's a pleasant sort. I'll enjoy squiring her
around." Alain paused, considering his choice and doubting
it. "You would like her. Isabella has taken her on as an unofficial protégé since her come-out last spring. She rides well
enough to keep up with the likes of us and her father has a
successful horse farm in Newmarket. She would be a grand
candidate for you. I feel guilty stealing your opportunity."

"Truly, Alain, we can't ruin Isabella's fun at matchmaking with such an easy solution," Tristan jested, sensing his
perfect plans about to be derailed by Alain's good intentions.
"As I said, Isabella can introduce me to any Eligibles." He

winked conspiratorially. "Women set such a store by these things."

Alain chuckled. "You are right." He slapped Tristan on the back. "I am off to find the fair Caroline. This is splendid of you."

Tristan assured his friend it was nothing and went off to find his own maiden, not that it was difficult since he'd already ascertained her position in the ballroom. Even if he hadn't known her location, he would have picked her out immediately. This evening, she was garbed in a domino of bronze satin and matching demi-mask trimmed in black feathers. The domino and mask were designed to match the bronze gown that peeped from beneath the cloak's folds. She'd chosen to come as Juno, Queen of the Heavens. Appropriately enough, Juno was the Roman goddess of women and marriage and whose festival originally fell on February fourteenth.

With the stealth of the wolf he'd arrayed himself as, Tristan came up behind Isabella and displaced the man standing to her left. "Good evening, my lady," he said in a low tone. He was rewarded with a slight start from Isabella as she took in his garb and deduced who it was that addressed her.

"What a surprise! Can we assist you in finding your Valentine? The Denbighs have been quite clever."

"There is no need. I have drawn your name, my lady." A subtle smile played upon his lips as he noted her shock.

"Indeed," Isabella said as the men surrounding her groaned. They had clearly favored her company over that of seeking out their lady for the evening. Tristan knew his arrival signaled their need to depart and let Isabella get on with the evening's venue.

"What shall be my first task?" Tristan asked as the men dispersed.

Isabella smiled up at him, her head cocked at a saucy angle while she contemplated him. "How did you get my name? There are a hundred women here."

Tristan spread his gloved hands in surrender. "There is nothing to suspect. Alain drew your name and I traded with him." He leaned closer and confided in a teasing tone, "I had to save you both from such a Roman liaison."

Isabella laughed and curtsied. "I thank you. Now, rescue me from the ballroom. I am too hot and I wish to stroll along the terrace."

The terrace was over populated with couples having the same idea. Tristan noted a well-lit garden path meandering towards a fountain. There would be nothing inappropriate about walking down there, where they'd be out of earshot of the ballroom but not out of sight.

"This is wonderful," Isabella exclaimed, stopping to sit on a stone bench near the burbling fountain. "The cool air is refreshing." She motioned for him to sit next to her. "Is there anyone you'd like me to introduce you to? I have some young ladies in mind, but perhaps there's someone who has caught your fancy?"

Tristan waved aside her suggestion. "Not tonight. I am not sure I would make the best impression dressed as a wolf." He reached behind his head and untied the ribbon holding his gray wolf's mask in place.

Isabella scrutinized the mask. "Who exactly are you supposed to be? I don't recall any 'St. Wolf' being associated with the holiday."

Tristan shook his finger at her like a stern schoolmaster. "Dear Juno, don't you know? February fifteenth is the Roman festival of Lupercalia. True historians credit this festival, not Juno's, as being the origin of our Valentine holiday."

"Ah, and Luper means wolf. You see, I remember my Latin."

"Wolves devoured flocks of sheep, so the people of Rome would pray to Lupercus to protect the flocks. It's a bloody holiday involving sacrifices and the like. Would you care for me to elaborate?"

Isabella wrinkled her nose. "It sounds perfectly abominable. I don't need to hear any more." She laughed, rolling her eyes skyward. "You've always known the most interesting things. How do you come by such knowledge?"

Tristan shrugged. "I read. I don't think I ever forget anything."

"What a handy trick that must be. I could use a perfect memory on occasion," Isabella said wistfully.

Tristan turned somber. "No, it's not as great a gift as you might think. I wish I could forget many of the things I know."

"The war?" Isabella's voice was full of empathy for him as she reached for his hand and squeezed it.

Tristan leapt up with a barely restrained yelp of pain on his lips. He clutched at his left hand, the one she'd touched. Isabella was beside him, concern for him evident in her warm eyes.

"What is it? Have I hurt you?"

"It is nothing, just a small problem I have with a nerve in my hand. My apologies for having alarmed you."

He should have known Isabella was too tenacious to let such a thing go with the flimsy excuse he'd offered. Before he could distract her, Isabella gently took his hand and stripped off the white glove. She stared for a long moment at the scar that bisected his palm and wrapped around his knuckles. The scar was hideous and stark, a thick white line against the tanned skin of his hand.

When she spoke, her voice was solemn. "How did this happen?"

"You don't need to know. Please, Isabella. It does not signify."

She stared at him for a long while before finally dropping his hand and granting his request. "Does it hurt much?" She asked, letting him cover the scar with his glove.

"I have some salve. As long as I don't overuse my hand it doesn't trouble me."

"Will it heal?"

"I imagine the scar will fade in time."

"I didn't mean the scar," Isabella said sharply. "I meant your hand. Will it heal?"

"Probably not." Tristan gave a wry smile. "But this is unseemly talk for Valentine's Day. We should talk of love, or at least of roses." He nodded toward the convenient but dormant cluster of rose bushes lining the garden walk. "Roses are the official flower of love, being the sacred flower of Venus."

"Oh, that is nicely done, my lord wolf." Isabella applauded. "You've managed to talk of both love and roses in one sentence while deflecting me from my desired course of conversation."

"Yes, so it seems that I have." Tristan patted her arm as she tucked it through his. "Let's go back inside and on the way I'll tell you about the *cartes d'amities* the French send for the holiday."

"Salud!" Crystal flutes of newly legal French champagne clinked in near unison beneath sparkling chandeliers as midnight heralded the time of unmasking in the crowded ballroom of the earl of Denbigh's lavish town house. People drank and laughed as masks were discarded. In one corner of the packed room, Tristan exchanged toasts with Alain, and the other two who completed their circle of childhood chums, Giles Moncrief, Chatham Somerset, and of course, Isabella. She looked delightfully disheveled without her mask and domino which she had laughingly discarded when the clock chimed and her cheeks were flushed from the warmth of the room. Tristan was so enthralled he nearly missed Giles's toast.

"Here's to our prospects of love in the upcoming year and to the return of Tristan. Our circle is complete again." Giles turned to Tristan, his voice booming amid the hubbub. "My old friend, we are glad you're home safely!" Giles raised his glass in salute to Tristan, who smiled humbly in the wake of his friend's enthusiasm.

Tonight, with all of them together again, Tristan could almost believe he'd never been away. His friends had embraced him with their usual warmth and they'd easily fallen into the camaraderie they'd shared in the past. A small smile touched his lips as he recalled how he'd met the four people that surrounded him now.

The four of them had grown up together on neighboring Lake District estates. When the three boys went off to Eton together, Tristan joined the group then through the fortune of being Alain's roommate. They had taken him in, joking that Alain needed someone with a decidedly English pedigree to balance out Alain's unfortunate moniker bestowed on him by his overzealous French mother. They'd immediately decided that nothing could be more English sounding than "Gresham." The bond between him and Alain had been sealed.

"I have long thought that masquerades became dull dogs once everyone unmasked. What's the fun of realizing you've just spent an evening with the same people you spend every evening?" Chatham remarked, using his height to scan the ballroom. "People are much more fun when they're someone else." Of them all, Chatham was the tallest, and the darkest, with coal black hair and keen near obsidian-colored eyes that missed nothing. Tristan long thought Chatham would have made an excellent reconnaissance officer.

Giles cleared his throat. "I knew you would say that. So, to preempt your impending boredom, I have arranged for something special. If you will all follow me?" He cocked a challenging blond eyebrow at the group, daring them to dispute his latest game.

Chatham groaned. "Whatever you have in mind, we'll have to do it here. It's positively a crush in here and I doubt there are any other rooms unoccupied at this point." He gave Giles and Alain a wicked wink. "Who knows what kind of decadence we may uncover if we go opening closed doors."

"Never fear, I've planned for that contingency as well. The only private place I could secure was the verandah." With his trademark efficiency, Giles ushered the group towards the row of French doors leading out onto the wide verandah overlooking the now dark gardens. There would be nothing to see out there tonight in the dead of an English winter. No one would bother them. They would have their privacy.

Tristan hung back, finding himself reluctant to engage in whatever scheme Giles had concocted. A tug on his arm indicated that Giles would not let him slip away. Giles had maneuvered back through the crowd to usher him along. "Come on, Tristan. I've planned this bit of fun especially for you. Alain says you're determined to find a wife." Giles winked at him and managed to deftly relieve a passing footman of two champagne bottles. Giles's deft antics made him laugh and Tristan found himself capitulating to his friend's well intended contrivances.

Once on the verandah, Tristan watched Giles settle them all on the wide stone steps, and pour everyone another glass.

"Let's get on with it, Giles. It's freezing out here!" Chatham griped, blowing in his hands and rubbing them together.

"Drink your champagne and stop carping," Giles scolded. "Besides, after the heat of the ballroom the cold is welcome." Then he got down to the business at hand, the surprise. "In honor of Valentine's Day, I have invited the lovely Irina Dupeski, fortune teller extraordinaire, to tell our fortunes in the hopes that we shall find success in amour." Giles finished with a grand flourish, introducing from the shadows a raven-haired woman dressed in luscious multicolored skirts.

"Your friends, my lord?" She asked in a Russian tinged accent, sweeping the group with a white smile framed by red lips. "Who shall be first?" she flirted.

"I am." Alain volunteered with his characteristic impulsiveness, thrusting out his palm as Irina settled on the step next to him.

She ran an experimental finger over his palm, caressing the lines. "What do you want to know, my lord?"

Tristan's thoughts drifted away from Alain's fortune as the gypsy's words were drowned in a wave of laughter from the group. He looked at each of his friends in turn and felt an all too familiar pang of loneliness deep in his chest. He envied them their closeness. He envied them the years they'd had together before his arrival into the tight-knit coterie. He envied them the last seven years he'd been absent from their presence, pursuing his own official and unofficial activities on the Continent for the Crown.

Tristan shifted his position on the balustrade where he sat, drawing himself further into the darkness, away from the shafts of light spilling out from the ballroom. He could see Giles, his golden head thrown back in a deep, honest laugh, his warm brown eyes sparking with mischief as he playfully ribbed Chatham. In a moment, the teasing passed. Chatham threw a warning look to Giles as Irina moved to take his palm.

Tristan sighed. How he'd missed them all! His self-imposed exile had transpired in a vacuum of loneliness. He'd missed Giles constantly organizing their entertainments. He'd missed Chatham with his distinctively soft, clipped aristocratic voice that women fell in love with everywhere. He'd missed Alain, his best friend, most of all. It had been too difficult to think about Alain without also thinking of Isabella—a very good reason why one shouldn't fall in love with one's friend's sister. He had learned that lesson too late.

Tonight, as Queen of the Heavens, she embodied the sun, dressed as she was in a high-waisted gown of bronze silk with tiny puffed sleeves banded in black velvet. Her honey-colored hair was piled high on her head in thick ringlets, a few trailing down to brush the almost bare expanse of her shoulders. Around her slender neck hung a topaz pendant which was designed to emulate the sun. He was filled with an unexpected and entirely inappropriate impulse to trace her body with his hand from the column of her neck to the topaz jewel that rested just above the swell of her breasts.

He shifted, trying to exorcise his growing discomfort. Seeing her yesterday had affected him more than he could have imagined. The incident in the garden had nearly unmanned him. The evening's festivities with their overt themes of love had done nothing to alleviate his situation. Isabella had been true to her word in assisting him with his search for a wife. She'd been by his side most of the evening, guessing at which Eligibles were cloaked beneath the dominoes. But not even the beauties she'd encouraged in his direction had been enough to distract him from her presence or the recent memory of her touch when she'd held his hand by the fountain. Tristan shifted again and made to slip further into the shadows but Giles's voice broke into his reveries.

"Tristan, give Isabella your domino, she's left hers inside. We all know you're a furnace anyway." Giles ordered with a good-natured laugh, referring to the inordinate amount of body heat Tristan managed to generate regularly, even in the middle of a winter night. Tonight, Tristan wished he weren't quite so hot-blooded. A dash of cold would be welcome to subdue his more heated thoughts.

The object of his ungentlemanly discomfort was indeed shivering, Tristan noted as he complied with the command, draping his cloak about Isabella's shoulders while Irina finished with Giles's fortune. He hoped everyone was too distracted by the fortune teller to notice the effort it took for him to make his action look like a casual gesture. His fingertips inadvertently brushed the exposed skin of her shoulder and he felt her stiffen at the contact. He wished he could see her face at that moment of contact. Did she shiver from hidden desire or from dislike? Had his scar repelled her?

Irina approached the spot where he and Isabella sat. Tristan withdrew hastily back into his dark corner behind her. He hoped the fortune teller would overlook him or at least have the wits to sense his reticence and leave him alone. He was not destined to be so lucky. Irina stepped past Isabella and took possession of his hand. "Such a handsome man must have a good fortune awaiting him." Irina flirted playfully, drawing him from his latest shadowy perch. He did not protest her inspection. He had not planned to participate in such a school boyish venture, but he was trapped now. He was only glad she had grabbed for his right hand and not his ruined left. He was not ready for others to know of his injury. There would be questions asked that he could not answer.

"Alas, a cold but loyal heart dwells within you." Irina fell silent, letting Tristan's hand go slack in her own. "I am sorry. You are blank to me." She turned his hand back to front and back again, studying the short, clean nails on one side and the multitude of criss-crossing lines scored deep in the palm on the other. The pretty gypsy furrowed her brow in puzzlement. Her eyes suddenly brightened. "Wait, there is something else here." She smiled up at him with dazzling white teeth. "You will find love soon. It will be a deep, abiding love that transcends all else." Redeemed, she let his hand drop back to his side.

Giles clapped his hands appreciatively. "We are all in luck tonight! What good fortunes await us all in amour."

Chatham held up a hand. "Don't jinx it, Giles. We still have Isabella's fortune to hear."

Chatham had meant it good-naturedly, but from his position behind her, Tristan could see Isabella flinch at the reminder. Was she also reluctant to have her fortune told?

Irina took the cue and studied Isabella's hesitantly offered palm. "Let's see, my lady. This is good. You have a long life ahead of you. You shall become a Grande Dame. What's this?" Irina ran a finger down a line creasing the center of Isabella's palm. "Love." Irina shook her head sadly. "This is not good. The line is troubled. You have loved intensely in your youth, but only for a short while and it has hardened you," she paused here for dramatic effect. "You fear love and all the things that accompany it. You caution yourself against loving again. But you must, or you will be doomed to spend your long years alone."

The other three laughed and offered humorous consolation to Isabella, but Tristan was not amused at all as he watched Isabella angrily snatch back her hand. She gave a gallant toss of her head and declared in what he expected was her best London-hostess tone, "La, Giles, you are not paying her enough. Fortunes are only supposed to be good."

"I think she must have gotten the fortunes reversed,"

Chatham jested as Giles took the gypsy off to handle payment. "Tristan is the least likely candidate to love hastily. If any of the fortunes are false, it is his. I think the fortune teller was overwhelmed by his pretty face." Chatham winked at his friend.

Tristan shifted into the light, displeased with the direction of the conversation. He attempted to come to Isabella's rescue. "How do you know? Maybe our little gypsy witch was jealous that Isabella was surrounded by so many handsome men?"

"Maybe it is all insignificant dribble." Alain spoke from where he was reclined on a stone step, looking as comfortable in the winter air as if he were lazing about in a summer hammock.

Tristan narrowed his gaze, taking in the mischief in his friend's eyes. Alain hadn't said much since the game had begun. He had his answer momentarily.

"Maybe all our fortunes are false because there is no such thing as true love. Valentine's Day is nothing but one gigantic farce." Alain waved his mask for extra emphasis. "I propose a test for love."

"Ho! A test of love, I've been gone too long." Giles sailed back into their midst and took up his position at Chatham's right shoulder. "We are agog with interest, Alain. Proceed."

"I propose a test to prove the existence of true love, or lack thereof and by doing so, proving the legitimacy behind Gresham's fortune." Alain offered, pushing up from the step and pacing the verandah as he outlined the wager. "I think there is no such thing as true love and all our fortunes are poppycock. Since Tristan's is the fortune which will be fulfilled first, we will use his as the experiment. As such, I will wager that Tristan doesn't fall in love and fulfill his fortune by the end of June. Any takers?"

"Do you take us for addlepated nincompoops?" Chatham said, deflated. "Tristan's not interested in anyone and he's been gone for ages. It'll take the entire Season for him to reestablish himself. The odds are against us."

Alain shrugged nonchalantly and pushed his hand through his hair. "On the contrary, Chatham, I think the odds are decidedly against *me*. Isabella has agreed to help Tristan find a wife and Tristan is eager to wed. Is no one game enough to test the fortune?" he asked again.

Tristan attempted to put an end to the awkward wager. "Alain, it seems no one is willing to take your offer. Alas, I am a poorer catch than I thought." He had meant it as a self deprecating joke. Chatham and Giles laughed but his words found an unlooked for champion in Isabella.

Isabella spoke up. "I will take your wager, brother. Our friend is a fine catch. I think he will fall in love by June and prove your cynical outlook false. If I am right, you are going to buy me the horse of my choice at Tattersalls." She beamed at her brother.

"Not that horse, Bella. I will never buy that horse for you. You know how I feel about the subject." Alain's voice was filled with consternation, suggesting they'd been over the subject before. "That horse is a menace. You could get seriously hurt or worse."

Isabella only laughed. "Then you'd better hope Tristan keeps his track record clean and doesn't fall in love."

Chapter Four

Muted sounds of the city at rest randomly pierced Tristan's self absorbed thoughts as he climbed the stairs to his Mayfair town house in the early morning hours. The clack of Alain's coach wheels on cobblestones faded into the distance as he fumbled for his house key. He was looking forward to a quiet glass of brandy to soothe his raw nerves. The evening had bordered on disclosures he was not ready to make and he'd been on constant alert not to let anything of his recent past slip. He'd only dropped his guard with Isabella and that had nearly been disastrous. He did not want her pity over a shattered hand.

He sighed and let himself in. The foyer was dim and empty. All the staff had retired for the evening, which suited his need for privacy. Tristan crossed the hall to his study and came to an abrupt stop as he entered the darkened room. The place felt disturbed. A chilly draft blew against the folds of his cloak. Silently, he drew forth from its secret compartment inside his cloak, the slim lethal blade he'd become accustom to carrying over the last seven years and spoke in a low, commanding tone. "Show yourself. I am armed and aware of your presence. I will not hesitate."

"Moreland, sheath that blade of yours. I am from the

Home Office. We have business to discuss." A gravelly voice intoned.

Tristan's eyes grew accustomed to the dim room and he followed the voice to the wing-backed chair near the window. He could make out the lines of a man's figure seated there. "Light the lamp on the table and show your face. Do not move from that chair." He commanded in a stern voice used to giving orders, although he did not doubt the truth of the man's claim. No one but his military superiors called him by his surname, Moreland.

A match flared. The wick of the lamp caught, revealing an angular face framed by thinning gray hair and distinguished by a long nose. Sharp eyes stared back at him. "Hello, Moreland. As distrustful as ever, I see."

"Halsey." Tristan said coolly, still alert to danger. He recognized the man. He had worked with him before. This was no ruse. Halsey was important to the Home Office. They wouldn't send him on a fool's errand.

Getting straight to business, Halsey extended a cream envelope marked with the official seal. "We have a simple but vital job for you."

Tristan raised a wary eyebrow. In his experience, those two words did not go together. No piece of vital espionage work was ever simple. He voiced his disbelief and broke the seal, scanning the contents as Halsey spoke.

"We've discovered information about the man who evaded you in France last fall. He's an English informant working for the French. We believe he has recently returned to England. The office would like you to serve as bait to draw him out. It's very simple, as you see."

Tristan gave an empty laugh. "He knows who I am. He's already exposed me. There's nothing I could tempt him with. He knows I am through with the game."

"You're wrong. He's only exposed you to himself. He's kept your identity quiet from others. We have reason to believe that you're the reason he's risked returning to England. Whatever is between the two of you has become personal to him. The informant is hunting you." Halsey let the last words hang in the air.

Tristan could feel the tic in his cheek twitch. "What exactly do I need to do?"

"Be yourself. Your exploits in Europe are legendary as an entertainer and womanizer. Now that you're home, announce that you're throwing a fete at your estate to reintroduce yourself to Society. We'll resurrect the 'secret admirer' ploy. If the informant believes you have information, he'll be less likely to kill you off. The informant will be bound to show up at the house party, thinking you're still receiving information coded in love notes. We are fairly certain the informant is among the *ton*." Halsey chortled and rubbed his hands together in glee. "Everyone will believe you. In the barracks you're known as a regular walking bacchanal, my dear fellow. The informant won't miss such a perfect opportunity to finish his business with you."

"The Home Office believes the house party ruse will work?" Tristan questioned.

"As long as you stay alive to give it. There's always a chance the informant will strike at you before you discover who he is."

The dynamics of the situation were not lost on Tristan. "This is to be my last assignment?" He understood perfectly how he was being used. He was live bait, which created an added incentive for him to join in the manhunt. One last mission and then he could put his career behind him.

"Yes and a good way to end your career, too. You're young enough to want a real life back, especially with the money you've got. No sense tempting fate and not living to make use of that fortune." The statement was about the most sentimental collection of words Halsey had ever uttered in his life, Tristan thought as he watched the agent disappear out the window.

Tristan didn't relax his stance until Halsey was well out of sight. Then he strode to the lamp and held the note over the flame until it burned. Finally, he collapsed into his worn leather chair and put a hand across his eyes. What a damn fine night this was turning out to be, he thought with sarcasm. Between Isabella discovering his injury, Alain's crazy wager and the sudden but perhaps expected news that his career was over, the evening couldn't get any worse.

He reflected on all that Halsey had said. Was Halsey right? Did the rest of the world see him as an immoral debaucher, to whom nothing was sacred? How ironic when he prided himself on settling for nothing less than a loving marriage—his very excuse for not having married yet.

He would marry for love or not marry at all. Of course he didn't shout that desire from the rooftops. His cover hadn't allowed him to. Tristan groaned. In France, his job had demanded he create an alternate identity. He'd acted the role of the socialite officer. He'd given splendid entertainments and spent most of his time convincing others he was nothing more than a buffoon who'd bought a commission in the army for the thrill of it, having no real leadership or military capabilities to recommend himself otherwise.

The ladies had loved him. He'd had a string of highly public affairs, many of which weren't real and others which were exaggerated—the most prominent being with the incomparable Beatrix Smallwood, the supposed widow of a cavalry officer but in reality his accomplice and partner. All of which made it easy for him to overhear or be the direct recipient of information he would not have been privy to if he'd been a serious military man. The affairs made it easy to explain his late night absences from his quarters on Rue de Madeleine.

Tristan groaned. If it was to be business as usual for this last assignment, Beatrix was bound to show up. He had hoped that when he'd left France he had also left Beatrix behind, along with the blurred lines between the fiction and actuality of their relationship. He did not relish the thought of explaining Beatrix to Isabella. He wasn't even sure it was possible to explain Beatrix without compromising the integrity of the mission.

It seemed that his alternate identity had become his reality. Halsey had said he just had to be himself. Be himself? If he were really himself, he'd be miles from London at one of his estates, burying himself away with his gardens and greenhouses. The real Tristan embraced nature, not man-made intrigue. The real Tristan wanted to live in the country with a wife who loved the same things he loved. But until then, he'd be stranded in London living out a ruse, as Halsey so eloquently put it, "as a walking bacchanal."

Three blocks away at Westbrooke House, Isabella stared helplessly at the pages of the book she'd brought to bed with her. The book was supposed to have guaranteed a quick passage into oblivion, but even with the long night of dancing behind her, sleep would not come. Her mind whirled with visions of Tristan. She replayed the evening in her head like a Covent Garden drama. His costume had been aptly chosen. He'd exuded a feral power that both startled and intrigued her when he'd neatly insinuated himself into her group of admirers. His polished manners had deftly dispersed them, leaving her alone with him.

Their walk in the garden had been most revealing. Isabella could not forget the horrid scar he bore on his hand or the naked vulnerability that had glinted in his eyes, if only for a moment, when she'd held the injured hand in her own and begged his story.

It wasn't the maimed hand that had been revealing, although it had been a shock of its own. It was the realization that the openness she had once associated with Tristan's nature was gone. She had not been conscious of its omission when Alain had brought him to the town house. She'd only intuitively found Tristan changed somehow. She'd passed it off as expected after such a long absence. But tonight when he'd adroitly steered the conversation away from his injury, she'd recognized what was different about him. Instead of cultivating mannerly behavior as a natural extension of himself, he was now using it as a façade behind which to hide his true self.

The book Isabella held slid to the floor with a thud as she recognized the full impact of such a choice. Tristan was hiding something and it was more than his injured hand, although Isabella had no doubts that his hand was in some way connected to the deeper issue. She yawned in frustration. She'd managed to solve one mystery regarding Tristan only to find another.

Isabella gazed down on the bustling street below from the long window casements of her chinois-styled front drawing room. She sighed wistfully. She'd be out there among the people of the city that morning if it hadn't been for her impending appointment with her dear friend, Amy Weatherspoon, Lady Briarton. She hadn't seen Amy since she and the earl had retired to the country three months ago. Amy would arrive within the hour, which left too much time to sit idly, yet not enough time to actually do something useful.

That wasn't exactly true, Isabella thought as she dropped the gauzy sheer curtain and turned to survey her salon, her eyes falling on the black lacquered escritoire across the room. She should take this opportunity to jot down notes regarding eligible wives for Tristan.

Isabella purposefully crossed the blue and white drawing room to the desk. Seating herself, she took out pen and paper, and separated the white page into two columns. The first column filled easily as she listed all the eligible girls she knew who were available for marriage. Tristan would certainly have a quantity of young women to choose from. It was the second column that had Isabella tapping her chin with the quill as she racked her brain for possibilities: how to woo Tristan? She knew it would not be enough to claim victory simply by having Tristan engaged by June. She'd have to prove he was in love. Additionally, she didn't want to see her friend merely betrothed. She would not wish a marriage of convenience on him. He deserved more. He deserved the fortune Irina had predicted.

The question remained: how to get Tristan to fall in love? What type of woman would he fall in love with and would love him in return? Tristan was a complex man. He would not fall in love with just any pretty face. The woman who owned his heart would have to be intelligent and caring, not to mention a neck or nothing rider with a genuine interest in horses.

Isabella stared at the names on her list. They were all respectable young ladies with impeccable reputations. With the exception of Caroline Danvers, she could hardly imagine any of them riding hell-bent-for-leather in a most unladylike fashion. Isabella grimaced and dashed a line through two names and then two more. Those girls would be as tempting as milquetoast. Tristan would not be impressed.

She sat back in the chair and sighed. This was going to be more difficult than simply finding wifely candidates. Names were one thing, courtship was entirely another. She could find girls for Tristan to marry. It would be far more difficult to find a woman for him to love, and she felt morally obligated to do that.

The muffled sound of the front door opening downstairs drew Isabella out of her quandary. Amy's musical lilt floated up from the foyer announcing her arrival. Isabella put away her plans and took a quick look in the ebony framed mirror hanging on the wall behind her. She didn't want Amy to suspect anything was plaguing her. This morning, she wanted only to hear about her friend's time in the country and perhaps to share the wager with her as a lighthearted lark, nothing more.

An hour later, over mid morning tea and delicately iced lemon poppy seed cakes, Amy burst out laughing, setting her pale curls to bobbing and the hand that held her teacup to trembling. "What a ridiculous wager! I don't see how it is possible to make Gresham fall in love. Who will you get to tempt him?"

"That's why I need your help. In the absence of any close female relatives to guide his choice, he has asked me to help him select a wife. If I could introduce him to the right woman, I can win the wager and Alain will have to buy me that horse."

Amy assessed her friend shrewdly. "For the record, none of us think you should ride that horse. There must be more to this than you're letting on. You're not the type to go to such lengths to win a simple bet. What's the real reason you're so determined to settle Tristan with a wife?" Her question was met with silence and Amy was forced to resign herself to inquiry. "All right, who's on the list?"

Isabella turned from the window and furrowed her brow. "That's the irony of the situation. I have names of potential candidates but no one with whom he'd fall in love." She strode to the desk and picked up the list she'd concocted with lines through the rejected candidates.

Amy studied the list. "These girls seem perfectly eligible to me. What's wrong with them?"

"I don't think they would pose much of a challenge for him. He'd offer them a pretty word and they'd swoon at his feet. He wouldn't fall in love like that." Isabella said with a touch of scorn to her voice. "On second thought, he probably wouldn't have to say anything. One look at his face and the girls would be begging to be his lady."

Amy stared hard at Isabella for several disconcerting seconds before offering a "hmm" and nodding her head. "Perhaps there are other reasons those women aren't good enough for him? Are there, Bella?"

"I can't imagine what those reasons might be," Isabella huffed, trying to appear disinterested in Amy's hypothesis.

"I can think of two reasons." Amy tapped her finger against her chin thoughtfully. "You fancy him for yourself, or maybe you're jealous at the thought of those other girls having a chance with him?"

Isabella turned away before Amy could see how close to the mark she'd been. "Stay focused, Amy. I must have a list with the right sort of names on it and to get the right sort of names, I have to determine why men fall in love to begin with."

"I don't think it is quite as scientific as all that!" Amy said, choking back her laughter. "You're not undertaking a great study."

"Do you know why? Why did Briarton fall in love with you?" Isabella pressed in earnest, ignoring her friend's blush at the direct question.

"He says I captivated him."

"How did you do that? I must get some paper and take notes. This is precisely what I need to know."

Amy did laugh that time, a gentle, sad laugh, as she rose from the settee and went to join Isabella at the long windows. She took her friend's hands in her own and squeezed them with affection. "The point isn't what I do specifically that entrances Briarton, my dear. The point is that men fall in love because they are captivated. What captivates any man is how he feels about himself when he's with you."

"So all a woman does is help a man fall in love with himself?" Isabella remarked cynically and offered Amy a frown of disbelief. "That's just what a man needs to feed his male ego which, as a rule, is substantial enough already."

Amy knit her brows together in concern. "Poor Bella. I forget you've not yet experienced true passion. Your cold heart worries me, my dear. What I meant was that a man needs to feel like he's the man he wants to be when he's with you, that he doesn't need to be anyone other than his true self." She patted her friend's hand in a way that made Isabella speculate as to how much Amy had guessed. She'd been Isabella's confidante since their debuts. Amy knew that while life with Westbrooke had been pleasant, it had not been a grand passion.

Isabella disengaged herself from Amy's grasp and resumed pacing, "Don't worry about my heart; it's not cold, just cautious. Worry about something practical like how my list of candidates is going to 'captivate'. What makes a man feel good when he's with a woman?"

Amy returned to her seat on the toile print settee and poured herself another cup of tea. "Perhaps a good way to think about what a man likes is to think about what you liked during your two seasons." Amy took a few sips of her tea. "What made you feel good?"

"Hmm," Isabella said as her thoughts unbidden recalled the way Tristan's long ago kiss had brought out the wanton in her; how she'd lived for the dances she shared with him just to be touched by him. Those were definitely not appropriate remembrances to share. Instead, she said vaguely, "Compliments. I liked it when my beaux would compliment my horsemanship."

"Men like the same compliments. Makes them feel stronger, sexier, and smarter than anyone else and they're potter's clay." Amy said airily, snapping her fingers. "I suspect they like it even more than we do. How often do you think a man is told how nice he looks, or how superb his clothes are? I told Briarton once how much I liked a certain waistcoat of his and he preened liked a peacock the rest of the day. Since then, he's taken much more care with how he dresses."

Isabella was skeptical. "I'll make sure only girls who compliment potential suitors are on the list. Really, Amy, that's no help at all. I can't guarantee these girls will know enough to do that."

Amy laughed heartily. "One look at his face and *they'll* be the ones writing poetry to *his* eyes instead of the other way around."

Chapter Five

February 27, 1816

Amy's advice proved to be unerringly true. The next two weeks, Tristan cut a swath through the remainder of the Winter Season. He was handsome and dashing with his best manners on display. He was courteous to shy young girls. He doted on the old dragons lining the ballroom chaises. At parties where men were in short supply, he danced every dance without complaint so that no wallflower was embarrassed by her lonely status. In short, he was too good to be true and the gossips, like lean wolves in winter, were hungry for fresh meat. They got a feeding frenzy at the Hampstead Musicale, the most innocuous event of the Winter Season.

Isabella went over her carefully constructed list of wifely candidates again before discreetly tucking it into her beaded reticule. She tapped her foot impatiently as the musicians at Lady Hampstead's musicale gave their instruments a final tuning before the concert began. The seat next to her was empty. Tristan was late, which added to her growing frustration with him.

She believed her plan to find Tristan a good wife was the closest thing to foolproof she could devise. She'd diligently researched the candidates' backgrounds. She put about feelers to see if such a suit like Tristan's would be acceptable so that he would not be hurt again by another father's rejection. Only when she was certain of the girl being open to Tristan's attentions did she introduce Tristan to the potential miss. When new families arrived in town, Isabella added to the list as needed. For all these efforts, not to mention the procuring of invitations to the fetes the girl would be attending, she had little to show for her endeavors.

For a man who had declared he was ready to marry and looking for a wife, Tristan was proving to be a challenge. The only candidate who received any regular attention was Caroline and Isabella suspected that was merely because she was in their constant company. For all his polite overtures, none of the girls seemed to tempt him. He'd rejected every one of the debutantes she'd shown him.

The grounds for rejection varied. One girl was too short, one girl too thin, another was insipid. One was overly bookish. One was not interested in horses. The reasons were endless. Isabella's patience was not. Tristan was being difficult and now he was late, not that she blamed him. Usually the group would have shunned such a gathering, but there were still few people in the capital this time of year and they had to settle for what entertainments they could find, even if it included Lady Hampstead's idea of an "Italian Evening," complete with the screeching wonder of a soprano from Milan.

The compensation for enduring such an evening would be a chance to introduce Tristan to another candidate, Miss Cornelia Hamilton, daughter of a wealthy and well-connected colonel in the Horseguards. Isabella had high hopes for this match. Cornelia was neither too tall nor too short. She was neither too thin nor too curvaceous. She was horse mad and she had a military background in common with Tristan. Isabella was certain there was little Tristan would find wrong with the lovely and versatile Cornelia. That was, if he ever showed up, she thought testily.

A tardy Tristan slid into the chair next to her as the first notes sounded. He flashed her a smile and settled in his seat, the tails of his coat perfectly arranged. If he'd arrived a few minutes prior, she would have scolded him for his late arrival. As it was, he'd timed his tardiness perfectly so that he escaped scolding. Isabella wondered if he'd loitered in his carriage or in the hallway on purpose. The best she could do now was to convey her displeasure with a look. She raised her tawny eyebrows in what she hoped was arch disapproval.

Tristan leaned over. "I am sorry," he whispered. "I had some business that could not be put aside."

Nothing else was said between them. They devoted their attention to the evening's venue. The soprano was second rate and the small orchestra backing her up was even more so. Isabella found it exceedingly difficult to focus on the mediocre performance with Tristan sitting beside her, their arms occasionally brushing as he shifted in his chair, a wooden folding affair that was too small to accommodate his broad shouldered build. His situation was not uncommon. Isabella noted on her other side that Alain and Chatham struggled with their chairs, too. Only Giles with his shorter frame seemed to find a modicum of comfort while the soprano screeched through a little known Italian aria.

Each brush of Tristan's arm made her increasingly aware of his physical presence and of her jarring responses to him. His touch was embarrassingly exciting to her. They'd touched often enough in the past weeks since his return: her gloved hand on his arm as they moved through the social events, his gloved hand against her back as they'd dance, his gloved hand brushing the bare skin of her shoulder on the verandah at the Denbighs' Valentine's masquerade. That had been delicious. She shivered in her chair at the recollection.

"Are you cold?" Tristan solicited in a whisper near her ear that made her jump. Her shawl slipped to the floor between them. Tristan deftly retrieved it and draped it about her shoulders. If she had been cold, the small smile he gave her warmed her thoroughly.

Isabella smiled back her gratitude. Inwardly, she reprimanded herself for such absurd behavior. She had to find Tristan a wife and quickly before she foolishly acted on her growing belief that she was falling in love with Tristan, again. She'd behaved rashly with him before at his expense. She owed him better than that the second time around. Besides, Tristan had made it clear that day in her parlor that he was home to seek a wife. He wanted her to help him find that wife, not for her to be that wife.

He wanted her friendship but he did not want anything more from her. In the last two weeks, he had spent a significant amount of time in her company. Not once had he behaved improperly or brought up the past. She should be supremely gratified that he'd forgiven her. She could expect no more than that.

The performance came to a blessed end. The audience offered their lukewarm applause. It was time to get on with the real purpose behind the gathering—to see and be seen. Isabella rose and shook out the folds of her delicate gown of rich ruby tissue, trimmed in gold around the high waist and hem. "Gresham, there is someone I want you to meet." She was careful to always call him by his title in public. It would not help his matchmaking prospects if anyone assumed there was something more intimate between them.

Tristan cocked an eyebrow at her. "Another candidate?" Was that weariness she denoted in his voice? Was that hope or disappointment that caused her heartbeat to quicken? Isabella steadied herself.

"Yes. I think you'll like her if you give her a chance. You have been a most reluctant suitor." Isabella scolded, placing her hand on the sleeve of his claret-colored evening coat.

Instead of keeping Isabella at his side, Tristan covered her hand with his own and turned so that they were standing face to face, a position that implied privacy in a room filled with large, chattering circles. "Isabella, I like all the girls you've selected. I just can't love them."

"Why is that?" Isabella asked breathlessly. There was little

distance between them. She could smell the betel leaf fresh-
ness of his breath beneath the clean scent of soap and spices.
His chocolate eyes darkened. His tongue ran over his lips in a
mesmerizing motion. He was going to declare himself. In a
moment he would say the words her treacherous heart had
secretly wanted to hear since the moment she'd heard his
boots on the hardwoods of her parlor: "Isabella, I love you."

The words did not come. Tristan's eyes narrowed as they
shifted from her own face to a point beyond her shoulder.
She felt Tristan's hand tense where it covered hers. Then she
heard the low sultry rumble of a woman with an agenda of
trouble masked in the purring tones of her voice.

"There you are, Gresham darling. I have been looking all
over for you. Don't tell me you've taken to seducing women
in the middle of a drawing room. La! That would take even
your audacity to new heights."

The woman who approached them was heart-stoppingly
gorgeous. Her raven dark hair piled elegantly on her head
showed off the gentle curve of her neck. Her expensive ice
blue gown was cut low to reveal her extraordinary cleavage,
of which Isabella noted, she was not afraid to offer Tristan
an advantageous view. The woman's deep blue eyes flashed
flirtatiously with Tristan as she snapped open her lace fan
and said with feigned naïveté, "I hope I am not interrupting
anything."

Isabella could not recall being so mortified by another's
behavior. The woman had no shame. If her outstanding
looks hadn't drawn the attention of every man in the room,
her insinuations about Tristan would have. Isabella could
hear the noise level in the room drop. No one was ill bred
enough to stare at them overtly, but no one was foolish
enough to pass up the chance to witness tomorrow's on-dit
in the making. Everyone was "looking" and everyone was
listening for what would be said next.

"Gresham, are you not going to introduce me?" The woman
said brazenly after Tristan glared at her for long moments,
long enough to make his displeasure obvious. Isabella

watched Tristan charily. The tic in his cheek twitched. Was his displeasure over the interruption or over her appearance?

"Mrs. Smallwood, this is the dowager marchioness, Lady Westbrooke," Tristan said stiffly. He'd made a point to only fulfill his obligation to introduce Mrs. Smallwood. A smile teased at Isabella's lips. Tristan had not assumed she would care to be introduced to Mrs. Smallwood. It was a pitiful victory, but she savored it nonetheless.

Mrs. Smallwood plied her fan coyly and laughed. "Beatrix, Gresham. Call me Beatrix. Darling, when have I ever been Mrs. Smallwood to you?"

The muffled murmurs of the room soared in volume now that the crowd had a name. Isabella studied the woman beside Tristan. Beautiful the woman might be, but she was all ice. The woman had no heart. "Gresham, how do you know Mrs. Smallwood?"

"We met on the Continent while I was with the army." Tristan's tone was cold.

The woman took the opportunity to slip her hand possessively around Tristan's arm. "He is too modest," the woman gushed, "have you heard nothing of his war record? He gave the finest entertainments while the troops were in Belgium. Brussels was never the same after he left. All the ladies could count Gresham as their special friend. He saw to it that none of us were left languishing, if you understand my meaning." She followed the last statement with a private smile meant ostensibly for Isabella, but those around them noted it as well.

The situation was intolerable. The woman was impugning Tristan's honor. Isabella had not risen in society as a leading hostess because of her blindness to the ways of the *ton*. Although her behavior as a widow was above reproach, she knew there were plenty of widows and husbands and wives in the *ton* who were not so circumspect in their morals. She understood perfectly what Mrs. Smallwood meant to indicate about Tristan. The gall of the woman was unbelievable.

"My Lady Westbrooke, if you will excuse us? I need to speak with Mrs. Smallwood privately." Tristan gave her a curt nod. His eyes beseeched her silently for understanding. Understanding of what? Understanding of why he had to leave her alone in the middle of the crowded floor to meet with this woman? Thankfully, Alain and Giles materialized from the crowd. She was not alone to bear the curious, covert stares of those around them. Alain took her arm. He spoke in a quiet, low voice. "Chatham has the carriage waiting, Bella. We'll take you home."

"Yes, that's a good idea. There's no reason to stay," Isabella said distractedly. She convinced herself that the whole purpose of attending had been to meet Cornelia Hamilton and that wasn't going to happen tonight or any time soon.

"Did you have to be so flagrant?" Tristan closed the door to a small parlor down the hall and turned to face Beatrix. The woman had a damnable sense of timing. He had been about to declare himself, to tell Isabella the woman he wanted to marry was her, not Caroline or any of her other candidates.

Beatrix dimpled. "I was right. I did interrupt something intimate." She gave Tristan a coy smile he'd seen her practice a thousand times on less suspecting men. "Is the most renowned lover on the Continent in love at last?" She softened her smile in an attempt to invite the sharing of a confidence. He'd seen this trick a thousand times, too.

"It is none of your business. It has nothing to do with the assignment."

"There was a time, *cherie*, when it was my business." Beatrix glided towards him, placing a knowing hand on his chest.

Tristan stiffened at the intimacy of her touch. "A short time, a long time ago. There is nothing but business between us now," he reminded her gruffly, removing her hand from his chest.

Beatrix smiled knowingly, seemingly not put out by his rejection. "Lady Westbrooke is your Isabella, is she not? She's the one who threw you over for the aging marquis. The one that drove you into the army." She guessed aptly.

She stepped forward again but Tristan was ready for her and moved adroitly to the fireplace, hands locked behind his back as he stared into the flames. "This is my last assignment, Beatrix. I am sure you have guessed as much already since you know about the debacle in October. The man who attacked me on the wharf knows who I am. I had hoped I might have given him a fatal wound that night but it appears that he survived. Since he still has a use for me, I am to be the bait to lure him into Halsey's trap."

"I know." Beatrix said simply. The warmth of her earlier tone had faded. Tristan found the cold professionalism of her voice reassuring. Beatrix was part of a past that was finished for him or nearly so.

Tristan did not turn from the fire. "I assume that your appearance on the scene means the roses won't be far behind."

"You assume correctly. It will be the standard routine," Beatrix affirmed. "My flagrant entrance will ensure that people will think the secret admirer is me once you make it known in the men's clubs that you have one."

Tristan nodded absently. "So the game begins one last time."

"So it does, *cherie,*" Tristan felt the caress in her voice, smelled her light provocative scent of violets, heard the confident swish of her gown as she passed him. Without turning, he knew when she had left the room.

Tristan drew a deep breath. Her interruption tonight had been disappointing but it had saved him from making a grand mistake. The game was beginning. The brief idyll of his homecoming was over. Danger was afoot. It was no time to be making declarations to Isabella. If he had spoken the words in his heart tonight, she would have become disillusioned before the week was out. At least now the flowers from a secret admirer wouldn't appear to be a betrayal. When the turncoat was caught and the assignment completed, he could explain it all to her.

Beatrix discreetly left the ball through a garden gate, undetected. Everyone had seen her leave the party with Tristan

and no one would expect them to return together. She doubted Tristan would even go back to the musicale. He was smart
enough to know that it would add credence to their relationship if it appeared they had retired from the party together.

The ruse had begun well and neither Halsey nor Tristan
suspected the double game she played within their larger
game. She had worried that Tristan might suspect something
but he was so besotted with Lady Westbrooke he couldn't
think past Halsey's assignment.

Beatrix climbed into the unmarked coach waiting for her
at the corner. A moment of jealously took her when she
recalled spying Tristan with the lovely woman in the drawing room. There had been a look about him she had not
glimpsed before. He'd looked handsome and noble, protective and honorable. What woman wouldn't fall in love with
a man who looked at her the way Tristan looked at Isabella?

She had known many men in her time. She knew Tristan
was a man worth having just as she knew she could never have
him. She'd set her cap for him once and failed to snare him.
Now it was payback time in more ways than one. Tristan was
about to face a well-deserved and long overdue reckoning.

The tittle-tattle started slowly with hints dropped at clubs
and by women visiting each other for afternoon tea. The
rumors escalated as the story of Tristan and Beatrix
Smallwood was told over and over at this rout and that card
party. Old military dispatches were dug out so people could
refresh their memories regarding the viscount. Scandal
mongers dragged out the Gresham family history, resurrect-
ing the story of his parents' deaths in an outrageous carriage
race. The gossip began to accumulate like a snowfall, starting as nothing more than tiny specks on the dark ground and
then overnight transforming into carriage stopping drifts.
One week Tristan was a nonpareil. By the end of the next he
was the rake of the century.

Isabella was beside herself. She had done all she could to
deflect the ill-effects of the encounter away from Tristan. She

reminded all who would listen that Tristan had made a point of not presenting the woman to her. Surely that suggested the woman was an unwanted nuisance to him. But there were too many other claims for which Isabella did not have answers. What had Gresham done during the war? What had the woman meant by her reference to his entertainments?

Isabella had her own questions and doubts. Had Tristan known this woman as more than a casual acquaintance? The woman had certainly suggested as much. If so, did he still care for her? She recalled Tristan's response that he liked the candidates she'd chosen, he just didn't love them. Didn't love them or couldn't love them? Why? She had thought it was because he might love her, but in hindsight she thought perhaps it was because he was already attached to Beatrix of the bountiful cleavage and cold heart. What did an honorable man like Tristan see in a brazen woman like that? Worse, perhaps he had meant to tell her about Beatrix that night at the ball. Like a silly girl, she'd thought he meant to declare himself when in actuality he'd been ready to let her down easily. She was mortified that he might have guessed her feelings for him. She'd tried so hard to hide her growing attachment to him under the guise of friendship. Apparently, she had failed.

Isabella poured out her speculations to Amy as they sat over tea at Briarton House five days after the scandal broke.

"You did the best you could, my dear," Amy comforted her. "Have another scone, you look wan. I am sure all this has worn you out. I suppose there's no hope for a match with Cornelia Hamilton now. What will you do?"

Isabella tried to show a lack of concern. "The scandal will pass by the time the Season is in full swing. He'll be presentable again by then. I am certain there is a large amount of misunderstanding mixed in with all this nonsense. All the nosy parkers who are whispering rumors now will be groveling for his forgiveness by April."

"And if not?" Amy replied in a cautious tone that hinted at more.

"What do you know, Amy?" Isabella asked suspiciously, setting down her teacup and waiting for the worst.

Amy lowered her voice. "Briarton told me that the latest rumor around the clubs is that Gresham has recently acquired a secret admirer who sends him roses on a daily basis with love notes tucked inside. Everyone speculates the admirer is the Smallwood woman."

Isabella looked at her friend triumphantly. "That's the biggest bit of poppycock I've heard in ages. Who started the rumor? I'd bet it's that idiot, Calverton."

Amy shook her head. "Briarton heard the rumor from Gresham himself, just the admirer part, not the bit about Mrs. Smallwood. That's everyone else's addition," she clarified.

Isabella was grateful she'd already set her teacup down or she would surely have dropped it, so great was her shock. Tristan had an admirer? First the rejection of the decent candidates she'd put together, then the appearance of the problematic Mrs. Smallwood and now the brazen secret admirer he flaunted for public notice. These were not the behaviors of the Tristan who had counseled her to make the honorable choice seven years ago. This new Tristan was a womanizer, a man of dubious connections and questionable practices. This Tristan had come home with a shattered hand and a murky past which he never discussed. What had her heart gotten her into? Isabella began to realize she didn't know this Tristan at all.

Late Afternoon, the Sail and Anchor Public House on the docks

The sounds of workmen loading and unloading drays in the dockside street were minimally shut out in the relative privacy of the dingy parlor she had frequented all too much in recent weeks. Her surroundings added to her growing irritability as she glowered at her partner. "You look too comfortable in such squalid surroundings. Used to slumming, are you?" she snapped as she shoved his polished, booted heels off the table. He was handsome enough with his sleek blond hair, but it was hard to believe he was a professional the way he'd dawdled this past week.

"I thought you had everything under control." The woman's eyes flashed blue fire as she paced the length of the private parlor at the inn. "I did my part at the musicale. I kept him busy once I got him out of the drawing room. I expected you to do yours. All you had to do was retrieve those coded love notes arriving in the rose bouquets from his 'secret admirer.'"

"Darling, there was some difficulty sneaking in through the back gate of Moreland's town house." The man tried to placate her with explanations.

She tapped him firmly on the chest with a well-manicured finger to emphasize her point. "Then don't sneak about like a common thief. You're a titled noble man; it isn't unlikely you might pay him a visit as a peer. Go in through the front door," she condescended. *Good lord, how difficult is it to create options?* He was exasperating.

He rose to his full height of six feet plus, his temper finally pricked. "Don't treat me like a novice, my dear. I am not one of your fledgling agents panting at your heels. Moreland and Halsey are on to us. We need to be careful."

"They are on to *you*," she clarified. "Moreland and Halsey suspect nothing unusual about my appearance or involvement. Still, that doesn't give you a license for sloppy work. We need to be quick." Her eyes narrowed as she looked up into his face, calculating her next move. She tapped her chin thoughtfully. "I could have Tristan take me home for old time's sake and afterwards, I could take the cards while he's sleeping." She got the result she was looking for.

He grabbed her upper arm forcefully. "Never. I know what you once were to him, but you're mine now and I will not allow it. I'll get the cards. In the meanwhile, I'll remind Moreland how dangerous I am."

She smiled coyly at his display of jealousy. It was good

he believed the tales about her and Moreland. "Excellent. I'll stay close to him and keep rumors of our supposed affair alive, in case we need other avenues of access to his town house."

He grimaced. "As long as they're just rumors."

She purred wickedly. "But of course."

Chapter Six

March 5, 1816

The house was beginning to resemble a florist shop in both look and scent. Tristan stood in the middle of the front hall, half dressed and more than a little annoyed at how roses were taking over his foyer and drawing room mantel. An arrangement had arrived everyday for the last week. He would have preferred something more exotic like the Turkish roses in his greenhouse on his country estate. At least, he supposed the roses he'd sent back were still thriving. He hadn't been home yet. But he'd done his job by bragging about the bouquets to any male who would listen for five nights in a row. He couldn't remember when he'd spent so much time in London Society. Surely everyone knew his "story" by now.

From the center of the bouquet he withdrew the card containing a coded message of moderate difficulty. Tristan scanned the card quickly before placing it back in the center of the bouquet. At least Halsey had been right about the simplicity of his role in the plot. He had only to leave the flowers with the card semi-visible on the foyer table or on the fireplace mantel in the drawing room with the other bouquets to attract the notice of anyone who might happen to call.

The untutored eye would notice nothing untoward about the cards in the bouquets. They would only see a novice's attempt at romantic poetry. An agent with training in codes would immediately see the beginnings of a pattern and the double agent who hid among the *ton* would attempt to steal the note. It wouldn't be a difficult feat to palm the note and slip it into a pocket.

Tristan's other part in the game was to get the play in motion. He needed to get the word out about his "admirer" and wait for the visitor to arrive. To get the rumor circulating, he had to tell someone, preferably a lot of someones. Beatrix's bold performance at the musicale had certainly helped. With word of the admirer spreading, everyone would assume it was she who sent the bouquets when in reality there was no one, just a trap for the informant. The sooner the trap was sprung, the better. He had not seen Isabella since the musicale and he chafed to set the record straight.

Tristan suspected the appropriate parties would get wind of his situation within a week, maybe sooner. Things would happen quickly from there on out. Thanks to the near-botched mission last fall, the double agent knew Tristan's true identity and knew that vital information had been passing through him to other agents in the field via "love notes" from a "secret admirer." Waterloo might be over, but there was still plenty of work for the government's secret agents. No one was ready to risk another escape attempt by Napoleon.

For all its simplicity, the "love note" tactic had worked exceedingly well given Tristan's cover as a gallant officer with a talent for romance. No one had questioned the amount of bouquets that found their way to Tristan's quarters on Rue de Madeleine. No one had questioned the night time hours he kept, supposedly sleeping in boudoirs other than his own. Then, after years of success, someone suddenly had.

A frisson of ice snaked down Tristan's back, unbidden as he recalled how close it had been on the Parisian docks the night he discovered his secrets had been betrayed. His ever-present stiletto had been all that stood between him and certain death. The informant had run bleeding into the night but he'd gotten what he came for, Tristan's identity.

Tristan knew that in his line of work that was just the same as being dead. Once an agent was known, his days were numbered. So he'd come home, not so much to die, but for the chance to live. This last mission was about his freedom. He'd find the man who posed a threat to his life and then he'd retire with as much peace of mind a former spy could have.

Seven years ago, he had not imagined such repercussions for his hasty decision to embrace a life of espionage. Some people drank away their mistakes, others turned to opium, but not him. He turned his agile mind to the all-consuming world of intelligence gathering. The foreign office established a cover for him as a modern day Lancelot of sorts and the world did the rest, spinning tales of his entertainments and *affaires des coeurs*. In the dangerous world of espionage, his good looks had been his coin and seduction his *lingua franca*. But it wasn't him, at least not the real him.

At first he'd told himself the deceit was part of the job, for king and country. His justification hadn't lasted long. At some point, his cover became his reality. He'd become what he had pretended to be. Only now, when he wanted so badly to find his way back to the light, did he realize how far he'd fallen into darkness.

He'd come home to Isabella and subjected her to the company of Beatrix Smallwood, an agent like himself. Compared to Isabella, Beatrix appeared coarse and unpolished. Seeing the two women next to each other served as a reminder that Isabella was not one of his war time conquests to be treated so casually. It also illustrated to him in the bluntest of fashions just how far he'd fallen. For all his handsome features, title and fortune, he felt himself nothing more than a beast arrayed in fine clothing.

He knew that was exactly how decent women saw him. After the rumors had started to fly, he'd come to understand that men found his sexual exploits worthy of praise, but women, at least the right sort of woman—the woman a gentleman married, found his behavior disgraceful.

Isabella was the right sort of woman. She'd fallen in love with him once before. Could he convince her to do so again? Persuading her to do so was at the heart of his plan to have her help him find a wife. He had not seen her since the debacle at Lady Hampstead's a week ago, but he'd heard of her valiant attempts to thwart the rumors. He hoped to show her through his gracious behavior that he was capable of being the man she once believed him to be, that this other man he'd become was a fiction.

Tristan laughed at the irony of his situation. He'd spent the last seven years seducing women based on the forbidden intrigue of his ungentlemanly behaviors, now he had to seduce the woman he loved by stifling those very tendencies which had been his stock in trade.

The bell rang, jarring Tristan from his ruminations. He answered it himself, startling Alain, who stood on the porch, his mouth wide open at such a breach of etiquette. "I hope you gave the butler a good reference, Tristan, and the valet too," he said dryly, taking in his friend's dishabille. Alain lowered his voice. "Is this a bad time? Is there a lady in the house?"

"No, of course not. No gentleman brings dalliance into his house. What kind of man do you take me for?" Tristan said irritably to hide his disappointment. He knew the answer already. Alain believed the rumors. It was a credit to his friendship that he believed the gossipmongers and had still lent his support by coming here.

Alain stepped inside and sniffed, looking polished and well turned out in buff breeches and an elegantly tailored jacket of deep green. "Lud, you weren't joking. This place smells like a perfumery. I had to come and see for myself. I know it's early but I've had the devil's own time trying to catch up to you this past week. You've been spending a lot of time at the clubs and hells. We've missed you at the more genteel entertainments. Giles and Chatham insisted I check up on you. Isabella sends the message that she can't help you find a wife if you're invisible. She's been quite chagrined by your absence this week; she takes her matchmaking seriously, you know."

Alain strolled through the black and white tiled entry hall looking at the various arrangements and stopping to study the latest one, fresh in the bowl on the round table in the middle of the hall. He picked up the card, looking at the bold hand on the short note. "Do you have any idea who it is?"

"No. And I don't particularly care. I am not interested," Tristan said curtly as he tucked in his shirttails and finished buttoning his shirt.

Alain waved a hand airily. "Don't get dressed on my account." He stopped in front of another arrangement of roses and fingered the card propped inside. "I would think a man who was hunting for a wife would be very interested." Alain squinted and peered hard at the card before continuing. "Of course, that assumes the secret admirer is a woman, Tristan."

Tristan looked up sharply from his buttons. "What do you mean?" He would have to send word to Halsey to get a different writer. If the notes were too obvious, the informant wouldn't fall for the bait. The agent would know it was a trap and Tristan would be dead. The hope of getting more information out of Tristan was the only reason the agent hadn't tried to kill him yet. At this point in the game, the informant had the advantage. He knew who Tristan was. Tristan knew only that the double agent was a titled English lord with a twisted sense of loyalty.

Alain crossed the hall and stood next to him, flourishing the card and doing his best imitation of the dreaded Professor Snodgrass from their Oxford days. "The handwriting on these cards is very manly. Women don't tend to write in such a firm hand." Alain held up the boldly scripted card for Tristan's inspection. "This person is trying too hard to be romantic. Have you read these messages? Women aren't so stilted when it comes to pretty phrases."

Alain chuckled and reverted to his own voice. "In fact, Old Man, I have to say this note qualifies as the worst love note in history and no doubt written by a rank amateur." He winked at his friend. "So you're even gathering virgins to your standard these days, eh Tristan? I was under the impression your discriminating tastes were reserved for the racier set alone." In spite of the teasing tone, there was a condemning quality underlying his voice that set Tristan on edge.

"Are you quite finished analyzing my love life?" Tristan responded querulously. He was in no mood to divulge the intricate truths and falsehoods of his life.

"No, actually, I am not," Alain replied in a vague tone that suggested his mind was hard at work on a problem, his eyes focused exclusively on the card in front of him.

Tristan swallowed hard, warnings sounding in his head from years of seeing conspiracy in unexpected places. At school, Alain had been a whiz at problem solving and puzzles. All the boys had been agog at Alain's ability to discern patterns and give them meaning.

"Tristan, I can't make it out instantly, but I think your fine admirer is sending you secret messages," Alain said in astonishment. "Which would explain the awful prose." Alain slapped Tristan on the back. "I can't believe you didn't notice, and you were a reconnaissance officer!"

"That's right, a reconnaissance officer, not a spy. I went out and surveyed enemy territory and troop placement before a battle. That's a little different than spying." Tristan said more tersely than he'd meant to. What he told Alain wasn't exactly a lie. Reconnoitering was different than espionage. He knew. He'd engaged in both.

Attempting a lighter tone, Tristan said, "Enough Alain. Give me the card. I doubt my admirer is smart enough to code anything. Let's go down to Brooke's and have an early luncheon." He reached for the card but Alain held up a hand.

"Wait, Tristan. This prose might not be very good, but there's a riddle inside, I swear it. The letters all occur in some type of order. Can I keep this and work on it?" Alain said gamely. "You can help if you want, it'll be like old times at school. We can pretend it's the latest math problem from Professor Snodgrass."

Tristan's mouth went dry as he considered the implications of his best friend's request. Could the informant be Alain? Was that why the Home and Foreign Offices had wanted him on the mission, to flush out his best friend? Who better to get close to the culprit than someone already close to him? Tristan's mind warned him not to draw rash conclusions, but his thoughts ran rampant.

"Leave the card here. I must confess I hadn't read the cards closely. I'll look at them later. If they stump me, I'll let you know." Tristan was all nonchalance as if the request hadn't seemed strange to him at all.

"Good, I need something to occupy my mind these days. Sommes is here with the rest of your clothes. Hurry up, I am starving." Alain surrendered the card good-naturedly and turned the conversation to other things as the butler handed Tristan a waistcoat and his valet hovered nearby ready to help with the cravat. "Isabella suggested that you come to the Burton soiree tonight. It's a political gathering, but several lords will be there with their families."

Tristan nodded at the suggestion, letting his valet fuss over tying a "mathematical" with the cravat.

Over lunch, he proceeded to brood, making the appropriate responses so as not to alert Alain to his distracted frame of mind, which kept returning to Alain's interest in the card. He tried to create a motive. Why would Alain be the informant? He didn't have any financial problems that Tristan knew of. Tristan doubted there were any. Isabella's marriage had restored the family coffers. Her wealth alone would keep them both comfortably for years.

Tristan knew men didn't inform for money alone, though. They did it for loyalty. What would be Alain's connection there? A rush cold of sweat turned his palms clammy. The baroness, Alain's mother, had been French. Alain had taken much teasing from the boys at school over the French origins of his name. Such a circumstantial link was ridiculous, the other part of his brain argued. There were several French émigrés living in Britain and absolutely loyal to the Crown. So far Alain had done very little to be considered suspect in this matter. A man searching for information and engaging in spy work would not be so blatant about his interest in the cards. Nor would he act as Alain had by calling his attention to the possibility of the verse hiding a message in code. A guilty man would find a way to secretly take the cards.

Still, Tristan knew from experience, one of the best ways to hide was to hide in plain sight. He had done it himself. That cover would suit Alain perfectly for this foray. For Alain, it was the perfect set up. He'd already laid the groundwork for Tristan simply handing him the cards. Tristan suspected that Alain wouldn't even need to remove the cards from his household. He'd just sit down with Tristan over whisky one night and talk him into translating the cards with him for entertainment. He might even invite Giles and Chatham over to do it and make a game of it.

That would complicate matters severely. There would be no proof that the agent was Alain unless Tristan told the Home Office. If he held off telling, it would be treason on his part. Could he turn Alain in? He thought about showing Alain the ugly scar on his left hand to see his reaction. He tried to rein in his galloping thoughts. He was getting ahead of himself. He wasn't even certain Alain was guilty and he had too little to go on to get worried over the coincidences . . . yet.

The Burtons' home buzzed with the hum of intelligent conversation punctuated by bursts of laughter from groups mingling in the various interconnected rooms. In the main salon, a room done up in the Egyptian style, Isabella held court under the light of a hundred candle chandelier, the flames catching the fire of her diamonds whenever she swiveled her head. Ostensibly, she turned her head to divide her attention between the various gentlemen surrounding her. Covertly, she used the opportunity to divine Tristan's state of mind. Her attention span was severely taxed trying to keep track of her own conversations while watching his.

He'd arrived twenty minutes ago and had yet to approach her. He was engaged in an animated conversation with Giles, Chatham and a few other men she knew by name. His relaxed posture and conservative evening dress did nothing to suggest that he was the target of much disreputable gossip. Anyone looking at him would not guess anything was wrong. He looked and acted much as he had acted prior to the scandal erupting. Didn't it bother him to be at the center of such notorious attention? Perhaps the lewd speculations didn't upset him because they were the truth? And perhaps he didn't care.

Isabella was both eager and reluctant to have him approach her. She wanted one thing from the evening, clarity. She wanted to confront him about the truth of the rumors so that she knew where she stood. During the long week, she'd wrestled with her thoughts and this morning she'd awakened with an epiphany. If the rumors were true, she could not in all good conscience let him pay court to innocent young debutantes. They would be helpless against his purported rakish techniques. She would not be a party to such one-sided matchmaking. She needed clarity on her position with him as well. Had he meant to declare his love before Beatrix Smallwood's interruption? She could not risk her heart without the truth.

Disappointed but convinced that Tristan was not going to materialize at her side in the near future, Isabella snapped open her fan and applied herself to the conversation at hand, hoping her court hadn't noted her distraction. "What of you,

Lord Driscoll, what do you make of Lord Burton's bill for the orphanages?" Isabella said as she turned to the fair-haired gentleman next to her.

The little knot of admirers chuckled and one of them spoke up teasingly, "Haven't you learned by now, Lady Westbrooke? If it doesn't have to do with horses or hunting, Driscoll hasn't a worthy thought in his head?" This brought another round of laughter, which Driscoll took good-naturedly. He spread his hands in defeat and used the opportunity to turn the conversation in another direction.

"It's true. Cunningham has the right of it." He smiled, revealing straight white teeth that added to his already attractive athletic looks. "I am more interested in horseflesh than any other thing or person in the whole of England, except my Lady Westbrooke, of course." Avery Driscoll gave Isabella one of his dazzling smiles while the laughter rolled at his own expense.

Everyone in Isabella's long standing court of gentlemen knew Avery Driscoll was head over heels for her, and Avery made no attempt to hide it, regardless of the fact that Isabella herself seemed oblivious to his intentions, treating him as nothing more than a highly esteemed friend. That treatment was part of her great charm.

As a young widow she had a certain amount of license to behave more freely with gentlemen, nonetheless she had never behaved loosely with any of the gentlemen who sought out her attentions. Consequently, her circle had grown accordingly in appreciation for her virtue. She had a reputation for treating men respectfully and fairly. She talked horses and hunting, putting them at ease with her conversation. Even if she had not been stunningly beautiful, men would have flocked to her by dint of her generous conversation. She did not toy with them or flirtatiously play them off against one another. She dealt with them honestly, each in their own turn. But no one mistook her for a manly woman who eschewed the more feminine pursuits of domesticity. Lady Westbrooke was unquestionably a lady.

"I say, Lady Westbrooke, I heard a rumor the other day that you were interested in Middleton's stallion," Driscoll continued once the laughter died down, turning his cerulean gaze on her alone.

"You heard correctly," Isabella confirmed, her eyes dancing as they had yet to do that evening. Nothing failed to spark her interest like horseflesh and she definitely needed a distraction. Her eyes darted back towards the door.

The collective gasp of worry mingled with disapproval from her group drew her back to the conversation in time to hear Darcy Prendergast elaborate on his concern. "You cannot be serious. Hellion? Why do you think Middleton is selling him? Certainly your brother is not thinking of letting you go through with it?" Darcy, always the stickler for propriety in the group, exclaimed with real horror.

"Prendergast is right, Lady Westbrooke," Cunningham put in, "the horse is called Hellion for a good reason. Middleton has been thrown at least four times and he's one of the finest riders I know. It would be a waste of money to purchase a horse you'd never get to ride." Of them all, Isabella liked Cunningham the least but beneath his priggish demeanor, he was polite and thoughtful which was why she tolerated him. Tonight his penchant for rightness was beyond the limits of her patience.

"Do you doubt my abilities?" Isabella said with a touch of steel in her voice that made Cunningham dart his eyes around the group for support. He was saved from answering by Alain's arrival.

"Gentlemen, I give you all a good evening." Alain nodded to the group, all of whom he knew on familiar terms. "I must beg your pardon and steal Isabella away from you for a few moments."

"What is it?" Isabella asked, slightly cross, as Alain steered her away from the group. "It had better be important, we were talking about Hellion."

Alain gave her a stern glance at the mention of the temperamental horse. "It's Tristan. He needs a break from the gentlemen. They're all sniffing around for another bit of scandal. Take a turn around the salon with him and cheer him up. Introduce him to a few young ladies. See if you can drag the truth out of him," Alain asked sotto voice as they reached their group of friends.

"Ah, Isabella, you look spectacular tonight!" Giles said effusively as the circle expanded to include the new arrivals.

"Thank you for noticing, Giles. It's new." Isabella looked down at the gown and fingered the sea green crepe of her overskirt appreciatively. "I had worried the round bodice would be too much, especially since it's not modish to wear much jewelry this Season. But my modiste insisted it would look quite the thing. I think she was right. I love the back." Isabella gave a small pirouette to show Giles the deep *V* in back.

"You're always beautiful, Isabella. The gown does you justice. I approve with your modiste's suggestions," Giles complimented.

Isabella gave a light trill of laughter and turned to Tristan. "Gresham, come take a turn around the room with me." Isabella extended a long white-gloved arm accentuated by a simple diamond bracelet fastened around her wrist. She placed it on his arm with all the correctness of an etiquette book. No onlooker would find fault with her request. No one would guess the rapid beating of her heart, that even such simple contact with Tristan affected her so acutely.

"How are you, Tristan? We've missed you this week." She kept her voice low to give them privacy as they strolled the perimeter of the room. She didn't look at him as she talked but rather to either side of her, nodding to those she knew as they passed.

"I am fine, Isabella. I've been busy."

"Alain said you've been at the gaming hells." Her tone accused.

"As I said, I've had business to look after."

His terseness stung. Couldn't he see that she didn't want to be shut out? Hurt, Isabella retaliated with a sharpness of her own. "We can try another topic of conversation if you don't like the current one. Shall we talk about Beatrix Smallwood and her performance at Lady Hampstead's? Perhaps you'd like to talk about your secret admirer or the atrocious stories circulating pertaining to your profligate habits on the Continent. We certainly don't have to talk about your work. Apparently, there are plenty of other titillating conversations we can have about any number of topics."

Tristan stopped walking. He gripped her arm and leaned close. "Stop it, Isabella. A shrewish tongue does not become you."

"I suppose it becomes me to be subjected to the indignities of scandal?" Isabella was outraged. How dare he scold her when he'd managed in one night to besmirch the pristine reputation she'd so diligently guarded since her debut? "Did you not realize how I would be implicated?"

The tic jumping in his cheek was proof enough that he'd known. He'd known. Had he cared one whit?

"I did my best to protect you, you have to believe that. I did not presume to introduce you." The grip on her arm tightened.

"And yet, it was not enough. I am implicated in something I know nothing about. I have a right to demand an explanation." She glared at the hand that held her fast as if noticing it for the first time. "Unhand me at once, you mannerless cad."

Isabella regretted her words immediately. Her momentary contempt was nothing in the wake of Tristan's provoked ire. He refused to let her go. Instead of freeing her, he ushered her through a set of French doors leading out onto a deserted balcony. The area was shrouded in complete darkness except where it was broken by an occasional spill of light from the main salon.

Tristan's manner was rough as he pressed her against the stone railing. "Unhand you at once? I think you mean 'undress me at once,' which I'd be glad to do."

Isabella shoved at his chest. "Tristan! What is the meaning of this? You've gone daft."

"It's what you expect of me, isn't it?" Tristan growled, stepping back from her, giving her room to breathe. His own breath came in pants. "You and Alain, Giles and Chatham, all of you believe the lies. That's what you really want to discuss, isn't it?"

"Are they lies, then?" Isabella said, hope inflecting her voice.

"You know me better than any of them, Bella. What do you think?" Tristan's voice was a whispered caress. It was the first time he'd called her by the old name since his return. Isabella thrilled to it.

"I have always known you to be an honorable man. In all your dealings with me, you've been nothing less. Let me help you. Tell me who Beatrix Smallwood is and why she'd want to disgrace you." She more felt than saw Tristan smile in the darkness. He stepped towards her, covering the small space between them again and gathered her in his arms. She reveled in the contact against his warm body even though she sensed his gesture conveyed only a great regard for their friendship.

Suddenly, his body tensed. He whispered an urgent warning in her ear. "Bella, we are not alone." He spun her away from the exposed railing and bore her backwards. A crash resounded on the concrete where they had stood moments ago. Straining her eyes in the darkness, Isabella could make out the shards of a large, pottery barrel, the kind used for planting flowers outside. At the speed it had been traveling, they could have been severely injured or worse.

"Are you all right?" Tristan ran his hands up and down her arms, trying to subdue the goose pimples. "You're shivering, Bella."

"I'm fine, just shaken a little. We could have been killed. What a terrible accident." She looked hard at Tristan. "It was an accident wasn't it?" Her eyes widened when Tristan didn't answer. "Tristan, what's going on?"

People flooded out of the salon, brought out by the crash.

Tristan had only enough time to whisper, "I cannot tell you, but trust me, Bella. Please," before they were engulfed.

Isabella was silent the entire way home. She answered Alain's questions about the incident with perfunctory answers. She was still trying to ingest the whole situation herself. It was difficult to give Alain answers when she didn't have any. One moment she was in Tristan's arms, albeit benignly, and the next she was being wrenched out of the way of a potentially fatal falling pottery urn.

The evening had been a failure. She was no closer to understanding Tristan than she'd been before the soiree. She had not gotten the answers she'd been looking for regarding Tristan. Instead, she'd gotten more questions. Tristan had confessed he could not tell her what was going on in the seconds before they'd been surrounded by the crowd from the salon. Tristan wouldn't tell her, but surely someone must know? Beatrix Smallwood? The secret admirer? With the scandal of Beatrix still swirling around London, there was no way she could approach Beatrix for the answers. But the admirer? She didn't know who the admirer was, but she knew who it wasn't. By Tristan's own admission to Briarton, the admirer was not Beatrix. The admirer had announced her presence a mere week or two ago, by Isabella's count. That was definitely too early to show oneself. It was possible Tristan didn't know who the admirer was and that the admirer hadn't shown herself.

A brilliant idea started to form and by the time she arrived at Westbrooke House, it had taken root. Isabella bid Alain a hasty good night and practically leapt from the carriage. In her bedchamber, Betty was waiting to help her out of the gown and assist her into her favorite silk nightgown and dressing robe in a soft pale rose. Isabella impatiently sat at her vanity as Betty took out the pins to her elaborate evening coiffure and proceeded to brush out her hair. Isabella's mind whirled, full of plots and plans for uncovering Tristan's secrets.

When Betty left, Isabella sat at her small white and gilt writing desk flipping through her engagements for the upcoming week until she found the one she sought. The Briartons' winter ball was in four days. Perfect.

Chapter Seven

The following afternoon

"**Y**ou're going to do what?" Amy asked in disbelief, nearly dropping the porcelain watering can she'd been using to sprinkle the geraniums in her conservatory.

Isabella looked up serenely from the potting table where she stood organizing seed packets. "You heard me, I am going to pose as Gresham's secret admirer. I have it on good authority from Alain yesterday over tea that Tristan has no idea who it is and he isn't interested in finding out. You've already told me Tristan told Briarton the same thing. I know he's not interested, but the admirer doesn't know that, so she'll be sitting around for ages thinking that if he's interested he'll track her down. If I intervene quickly enough, no one will be the wiser. The admirer, whoever she is, will think he wasn't interested and just fade away, not guessing that someone took her place."

Amy shook her head disapprovingly. "Won't it be obvious that the admirer is you? How could he *not* recognize you?"

Isabella grinned. "I am way ahead of you on that. It would work in the dark. With heavy veiling and gloves, it could be anyone."

Amy looked squarely at her friend, who was suddenly overly absorbed in sorting seeds. "Why are you doing this?"

"Tristan is in danger and he won't confide in anyone." Isabella lowered her voice to a whisper. "The crashing pottery was not an accident, Amy. Someone wanted to send a message of a very deadly nature. I am sure of it."

"I think you might be reading more into the situation than it warrants. One falling pot does not an assassination make," Amy said skeptically. "I am more interested in why you were out on the balcony alone with him."

"What a nosy parker you are!" Isabella scolded her friend. "If you must know, we were quarreling about the rumors." She set a clay pot down with such force that the seeds jumped from their carefully appointed places and mixed together. "He says the rumors about his decadence are lies. If that's true, then he's definitely hiding something. If it's not true, then a jealous husband is probably hunting him down. Either way, Tristan is in trouble and I intend to find out why."

"If you're set on posing as the admirer, when do you plan to make your appearance?"

"Soon." Isabella answered vaguely, recognizing too late that the ambiguous answer would set off warning bells for Amy.

"When?"

"The night of your winter ball." Isabella admitted.

Amy groaned. "I was afraid of that."

Isabella smiled reassuringly at her friend. "Don't worry, I have everything under control."

The Sail and Anchor

"You nearly killed him last night with your pottery urn stunt!" The strikingly attractive woman managed to keep her anger to a polite whisper at the sight of her accomplice entering the private parlor.

The man was impeccably dressed and in high spirits. He

was undaunted by his partner's outburst. He merely smiled in the wake of her ire. "I knew what I was doing. You want him to feel hunted, no? Now he's got to watch out for himself *and* the dowager. You know, the marchioness complicates matters."

The woman began to pace. "He's besotted with her. In the end, she will prove a useful distraction. She will blind him to the realities around him until it is too late. The irony is that he's asked her to find him a wife. She hasn't any clue he's already found one and it's her." She gave a cold laugh.

"Do I detect jealously?" The man asked with an edge to his voice.

"I finished with Moreland the night he killed my brother on the Paris docks."

"Does he guess the real informant is dead?"

"No. He thinks we, or rather you, are the genuine article. So does Halsey," she said with grim satisfaction.

"Should I take that as comforting?"

"As long as it assures our success," she gave a sly look. "You aren't the only tall, blond-haired man amongst the *ton*. We could get lucky and keep Moreland looking in the wrong places. He may even point the finger at the wrong person, all for the sake of patriotism. You know how honorable Moreland is."

Four nights later at the Briartons' Winter Ball

Tristan cultivated an air of negligence, lounging against one of the columns lining the Briartons' tasteful Greek styled ballroom. He took in the room, blazing with candles and swathed in elegant yards of navy blue fabric studded with brilliants to resemble a clear winter sky. No one watching him would suspect from his indolent posturing that his mind was speeding through the evening's possibilities. In his waistcoat pocket was a well-thumbed card. The little intrigue to catch the informant had taken an unforeseen turn that afternoon with the arrival of the waistcoat he now wore.

The "secret admirer" wanted to meet with him tonight. How curious, when he knew there wasn't really an admirer at all. Someone dared to play the imposter. He wondered whom? Could it be the double agent himself arranging this rendezvous? That made little sense since the agent already knew whom Tristan was and what Tristan possessed—the supposed information. In any case, the informant knew an admirer didn't exist. Perhaps the agent had figured out the information was false? In that case, the agent would want to seek him out for the sole purpose of killing him. He wouldn't need to go to such elaborate efforts. Most likely, it was some daring woman of the *ton* who thought to amuse herself by posing as the admirer.

Whoever she was, she had excellent taste in clothing even if she was interfering in his plans. Tristan looked down at the elegant celery waistcoat he wore with its placard of silver buttons. He had been completely taken by surprise when the package had arrived that afternoon bearing the markings of an excellent men's tailor on Bond Street.

Tristan fingered the silver watch chain with its discreet emeralds placed every fifth link. Although the waistcoat was stunning enough for evening wear, Tristan had been compelled to wear the garment regardless of his personal inclination. The card accompanying it had been succinct in its demands. It had read, "If you are willing to meet, wear the waistcoat. I'll be among the guests this evening at the Briarton Winter Fete."

Even so, his own code of honor allowed him no alternative. He had no choice but to meet with her tonight and warn her off. It wouldn't do to have an innocent accidentally involved in the Home Office's plots. Tristan was certain a woman had sent it—a daring woman who knew she was not the admirer and who knew him. She knew him very well to order such a tailored waistcoat with the surety that it would fit him. She had to have known the waistcoat's late arrival would not leave time for alterations before the ball.

His thoughts turned to Beatrix. She had the means, the taste and the knowledge of him to have selected the vest so accurately. But she had no motive. She had public access to him. Already the town buzz gave out that he and Beatrix had resumed their continental affair. Besides, she would not risk any action that would compromise the mission. Beatrix was a professional in all things related to love and war.

He understood the need for Beatrix's presence in this last game, but he did not welcome it. Beatrix's appearance had single-handedly wrecked his progress with Isabella. Whatever he'd gained back in terms of her trust the night of the Burtons' soiree would be sorely hindered by the escalating tattle surrounding him and Beatrix.

Tristan sighed. He was not making progress where Isabella was concerned, unless he counted driving himself mad with the wanting of her. He had not seen her since the incident at Burton House. Since then, he'd been plagued by his growing dilemma. What was the best way to protect Isabella? Should he keep her close so he'd be able to bodily protect her should the double agent attempt to target her as a warning to him? Or should he put her as far from him as possible and protect her through his absence?

At the sound of heightened gaiety, Tristan's dark gaze turned to survey the entrance to the ballroom. His eyes narrowed at the sight filling the archway. Isabella and her entourage had arrived. Tonight she was accompanied by her brother Alain, Chatham, Giles and the ever-present Avery Driscoll, who was classically dressed in evening black relieved only by a cream satin patterned waistcoat and looking undeservedly elegant.

Giles caught sight of him and Tristan watched him steer the group in his direction. With a stab of envy, he studied Isabella with Driscoll. They made a striking pair with their graceful physiques as they walked in the center of the group. But Isabella was unmistakably the bright, shining core. Driscoll was merely a foil for her brilliance.

For the ball, she was dressed in an oyster-colored gown of

ivory crepe over a velvet slip of matching ivory. She was bejeweled simply in pearls. The gown swished luxuriously as she moved. The deep folds of the skirt emphasized the soft, expensive richness of the gown, giving Isabella the look of an ethereal goddess. The only hint of color in the ensemble was the red rose she wore tucked behind one ear, matching the deep red gros grain ribbon that trimmed the high waist and sleeves. For a moment, he was struck by the peculiarity of the rose. It wasn't like her to wear flowers in her hair. Usually, Isabella preferred to weave strands of pearls through her coiffure.

Tristan bowed as the group approached. He greeted everyone, but he was eager to get Isabella alone. The orchestra began to play again after their short break from the first set. The second set began with a waltz. He could not have asked for a better number. "Isabella, would you care to dance with me?" He asked hastily, aware that Driscoll might try to claim the honor. His instincts were not wrong. A glance at the other man indicated his surprise. Isabella quickly looked between the two men. She murmured something placating to Driscoll before turning her attention to him.

"I would love to dance, Gresham."

Tristan savored the feel of her lithe form in his arms as he swung them through the first turn. He wanted nothing more but to enjoy dancing with her. It had been ages since he'd danced with her at her debut, back when the world was rosy and his path had seemed so clear. But he knew the dance would not last forever. He would not get another chance to have her alone before his unwanted assignation with the "secret admirer."

"Are you well, Bella?" He searched her face for anything she might be hiding.

"Yes. You are well? Did everything get sorted out after the accident at the Burtons? I was sorry to leave you to manage it on your own." She turned her warm gaze on him intently. It seemed that she was searching for signs of hidden meaning as well.

"I am fine. Thank you for your concern." How long had it been since someone had genuinely cared for his safety with no other ulterior motive?

"Tristan, you must tell me what is going on. I know the incident was no accident. Someone tried to harm you."

"Dear Bella, I cannot tell you and you are safer for not knowing. In a few weeks, it will not even signify." He smiled as kindly as he could, hoping to convey how sincerely he meant the words. He knew Bella's tender heart would be hurt by the rejection. He was surprised that the tenacious Bella simply nodded and accepted his statement.

The waltz ended and he returned Bella to the group, or what remained of it. Chatham and Alain had sauntered off somewhere, most likely the card rooms. He pulled out his pocket watch and ascertained the time.

"An appointment, Gresham?" Driscoll asked pointedly.

Tristan glared at him. The man wanted to call Bella's attention to his departure. No doubt, Driscoll wanted to make something sordid out of his need to leave. "I promised to meet someone." He met Driscoll's gaze with an even stare of his own. He'd learned long ago that the best way to manage difficult situations was with the truth. Ironically, no one expected him to come out with the truth so they were usually stunned into silence. He was pleased to note that the righteous Driscoll was no different. He pulled out his silver watch once more and made a show of checking the time again. "If you'll excuse me?"

Tristan knew he was early for the rendezvous as he strode out to the quiet conservatory. Experience taught him it paid to be early, to have a chance to become aware of all the entrances and exits possible from a location. He'd have preferred having a witness secreted away behind the potted plants too, just in case, but there had been no viable candidate, so he had come alone to survey the conservatory and wait.

Tristan smiled appreciatively in the darkness as he closed the French doors behind him. The conservatory was the

ideal meeting place for his admirer. The room was fragrant
and fresh, offering a cacophony of scents mingled with the
discreet trickle of fountains placed around the large room.
As his eyes grew accustomed to the darkness, Tristan made
out a rattan sofa set near one of the putti-spilling-water-
from-a-jug fountains. There were only two ways in and out:
the door he'd used from the hallway and another door leading in from the yard. Satisfied with his efforts, Tristan sat
down on the sofa to wait. The soft sounds of water tempted
him to relax and give into this sensory paradise, but his training demanded vigilance, so he stayed alert, one hand ready
to draw his hidden blade at the first sign of disaster. Tristan
felt his muscles tense as the French doors opened and a
darkly clad figure swept in. With an ease that discomfited
him, Tristan slipped into the role he'd become so well
known for in his covert circles—the dangerous seducer.
Whoever this person was, woman, assassin or both, he was
ready on all accounts.

"Be at ease, milord," the figure said in a low feminine
tone. "It is I with whom you are expecting to meet." She
came forward, all veil and cloaking, to stand in front of him,
full of her own confidence. "I am pleased you have come."

Tristan's other senses were primed since his sight was
limited. He could smell her as she stood in front of him.
Her perfume was a rosy floral scent cut with vanilla. He
thought fleetingly of the fragrance of Isabella's rose this
evening as they'd danced. His heart leapt strangely in his
chest before he discarded the notion. No, he had left Isabella fuming in the ballroom. Besides, there was vanilla in
this scent, too.

He could feel the expensive weight of her cloak folds
against his leg. She was bold. He knew that already. No
woman ever sent a man a piece of apparel. No woman dared
to meet with a man alone at her own instigation. No woman
dared to play imposter. This woman knew she wasn't the
secret admirer of whom he'd been bragging about all over
town. But this woman dared all of these things. Now she

radiated a mysterious sensuality by keeping herself covered from him in all her veiled trappings while letting him know her through his other senses, an erotic bit of irony.

In his own low, seductive tone, Tristan asked, "For what have we come?" He reached a hand up to caress her cheek through the veil. She grasped his wrist and waylaid his hand.

"I could not stay away. It was no longer enough to admire you from afar and honor you with gifts." Her tone was sultry as she turned over his captive right hand and began to trace his palm with her gloved finger.

Oh she was bold! Claiming the roses were from her when she knew no such thing was possible. Tristan smiled in the dark at her audacity. He knew how to play this game. A few fine words and he would have her veil off and who knew what else. "I have enjoyed your attentions. The flowers are exquisite and the waistcoat is of the finest. I am honored and flattered by your desires." He paused for good effect. "Let us have no more secrets between us. Let me see your face." His voice was near her ear, his breath feathering the veil. There was no longer any distance between them. He expected compliance after his sweet words and he made to gently raise the veil only to be forestalled once more by her hand. Did he imagine that she trembled? He was struck by the odd mixture of knowing womanhood and virtue in her behavior. Her words were practiced and coy. Yet her actions belied the confidence with which they were spoken.

"I think the game has been enjoyable for us both, sirrah. Perhaps we should prolong our game by altering the rules. Truly, I am no longer a phantom to you. You smell me. I feel your body as it touches me, learning me bit by bit without actual sight. I am no longer a stranger. I think that is revelation enough for one evening."

"How shall this game be played, then?" Tristan asked in a near whisper. He was not without his wits or weapons when it came to seduction. He captured the hand she had used to stroke his palm and placed his lips in its silken center. He moved his fingers to the pearl-buttoned length of the glove and deftly began flicking the buttons open, offering kisses along the newly bared expanse of her arm.

When she resisted and drew back, Tristan held her hand tightly. "My dark lady, you should know that too much resistance spoils the game. I must have some compensation, some show of favor if I am to be encouraged to continue." He brought his head up from its ministrations at her hand, a twinkle of charm in his eye if anyone could see it. "Besides, my dark angel, there is no fear of revelation from a simple arm being bared. I can hardly see it. I sincerely doubt I would be able to note any telltale marks or signs that would give away your identity." With that, Tristan pulled the glove off and proceeded to draw small, tantalizing circles on her bare palm.

He smiled as he pressed a thumb to the base of her wrist and felt the speed of her pulse. She was more affected than she let on. He was pleased. He would hate to disappoint her after her "admiration from afar." Lowering his head, he offered her wrist a gentle kiss. "I do not disappoint you, I think," he flirted boldly.

She replied with equal bluntness. "No, my lord, you do not. I am pleased." Then she grasped his hand and held him away from her, stepping back, putting distance between them. "I must go now, before I am missed. We will meet again."

Coolness stole into Tristan's voice. "If there is a next time, what shall we do? Shall I see your face?" He did not like being played with, and she was playing now. Once she had stepped away from him, he had lost his power to equalize their roles. He saw clearly that she was using her departure to set the rules to her advantage.

"I do not think you shall see my face yet," she said coyly, turning to leave and cut off the conversation. "We shall talk and get to know each other."

Tristan closed the distance between them in two rapid steps. "Be warned, this game of secret identity is a dangerous one. You do not know with whom you play." He growled. If she'd listened to the rumors about him, she would expect something more from him. He couldn't afford to expose his cover just yet. It would not suit for this woman to spread rumors that she had bested the notorious viscount. "I will have my due for this night's work."

Lightening quick, Tristan reached for her and pressed her against him, one hand about her waist, another at the back of her neck as he brought her lips to his, the veil between them. His kiss was ferocious and demanding. With satisfaction, he felt her respond to his force, nipping at his lower lip as best she could with the filmy material as a barrier. He had meant to show her his power, but her hungry response had leveled the playing field.

She broke the kiss first with a flirting lilt. "We shall have a grand passion between us in time, my impatient one." But there was a slight tremor to her voice as she spoke before she turned and fled.

Isabella's shaking form barely got her to the little chamber she had used earlier to change into her disguise. She collapsed on the narrow cot. Emotions surged through her. Volatile was the only way to describe what had transpired between her and Tristan in the conservatory. The encounter had started well enough. For the most part, she had managed to keep the upper hand and discourage any further revelation of her identity. She'd learned plenty from the encounter, but not all of it was to her liking.

Tristan had told her the rumors were lies but his behavior tonight had clearly proven otherwise. That bit he did with her hand, caressing it and divesting it of its glove and then kissing it had literally sent ripples of sensual delight up her spine. Alone, the singular move would send most women into a pleasure-driven swoon. Coupled with his low voice conveying hot intimacy in every tone, it was a recipe for irresistibility. Tristan's farewell kiss had nearly been her undoing. It wouldn't happen again, she reasoned, putting the rose back into her hair and smoothing her coiffure. Of course, that assumed there would be a second time.

She began to strip off her disguise and halted with horror. The black glove was gone. Tristan had kept it. He'd probably planned that move deliberately to be left with a token of her visit. What would he do with it? Would he try to blackmail her into revealing her identity? That didn't make sense. He couldn't blackmail her without knowing her. Still, she didn't like the thought of him possessing the glove, especially knowing what she knew now.

In hindsight, she was thoroughly scandalized by the way she'd acted and reacted in the conservatory. Her cheeks burned with her indiscretion. Had she really said such things? In all her grown life, she had never behaved in such a flagrant manner, nor had a gentleman acted so forward with her. Tristan's behavior was no less than she deserved. The kind of woman who bought men clothing and arranged to meet with them in dark places could only expect to be treated the way Tristan had treated her. But, dash it all, he didn't have to be so very good at it.

Common sense dictated she should call off her charade, but then she'd not get the answers she needed to the remaining question: what had Tristan been doing on the Continent all these years? Tonight had proven he hadn't been soldiering, at least not in the nominal sense. She'd bet whatever it was had something to do with the attack at the Burtons.

The thought of the attack caused Isabella to strengthen her resolve. Tristan was in danger. He needed help even if he admitted it or not. There was no other avenue left for her to use in order to get close to Tristan. In the old days, it would have been easy enough to ask Tristan outright and he'd have told her. But those days were far behind them. Tristan needed her. She would not turn hen-hearted because of one kiss.

Chapter Eight

The ball was at its zenith when Isabella returned to the party. Avery Driscoll was waiting for her and she headed straight for the safe harbor of his presence. Peripherally, she noted Tristan enter the ballroom from a door near the balcony. She hoped he wouldn't join them. She was not ready to encounter him yet. To ensure that didn't happen, she smiled winningly at Avery. "Shall we stroll? I believe you mentioned earlier you had some news to share with me?" Not even Tristan would dare to interrupt a tête-à-tête between two close friends.

Avery Driscoll visibly brightened and inclined his golden head in acceptance. "I do indeed have news that should appeal to you," he began as they walked slowly among the crowd. "I have completed the purchase of the stud farm not far from your place in Newmarket."

"Congratulations, that is wonderful to hear." Isabella was genuinely happy for him. Avery Driscoll knew horses as well as she. He was an expert rider and had a solid eye for prime horseflesh. Avery continued to look at her meaningfully. She had the maggoty notion that the announcement was a prelude to a more personal conversation.

Avery placed his other kid-gloved hand over hers where it lay on his sleeve. "I am glad you're thrilled. I am over the moon about it. I think you know it has been one of my grandest dreams to establish a superior breeding program. The price was substantial but it did not beggar me. I am looking for a stud. I have my eye on Hellion, Middleton's stallion." Isabella began to protest when he raised a hand in mock surrender. "Don't cut up at me, let me finish. I know you have designs on that horse for yourself. I am hoping we'll be able to come to an amicable agreement."

Isabella gave a merry laugh. "Absolutely, as long as Hellion is mine, I will support you completely." The look on Avery's face was priceless. He did his best to hide his consternation at her literal answer and Isabella knew he'd meant something more by his reference to an "amicable agreement."

"Lady Westbrooke, may I ask you a bold question?" He'd returned his hand to cover hers again. Isabella barely hid her frustration. The persistent man was going to try again. She liked Avery Driscoll immensely. She had no desire to hurt his feelings. She nodded politely.

"Lady Westbrooke, I have heard the buzz about town regarding the flagrant proclivities of Viscount Gresham. Usually, I believe a man's business is his own but in this case, he has implicated you directly. As someone who cares deeply for you, I find I must ask the nature of your relationship with the viscount."

Isabella wished she could answer that question. How could she explain her relationship with Tristan to someone else when she couldn't explain it to herself? The response she gave Avery was as decorous as his request. "Viscount Gresham's proclivities, as you delicately put it, are indeed his own to manage. I daresay in time, the truth will come out and those who spread the vicious lies will recant. As for my relationship with him, Gresham has been a long time friend of my brother's. They were chums at Eton, you know. Gresham spent several school vacations at our place."

Avery took too much hope from the neutral message. "I

am gratified to hear that. I feared it might be otherwise. Now that the business of the stud farm is completed, I would like to call on you so that we can discuss other business— another grand dream as dear to me as the horse farm."

Isabella did her best to fob him off. "As you wish, Lord Driscoll. Tonight I have no more head for business. I would like to return to my brother and have him see me home."

Avery was efficient and devoted. Alain was eager to leave. Between them, they had Isabella ensconced in the Wickham carriage in no time. Isabella closed her eyes and sank back against the seat. The evening had been more wearying than she'd anticipated.

The squabs groaned as Alain settled across from her in the rear facing seat. "So, am I to anticipate a visit from Driscoll in the morning?"

Isabella's eyes flew open. "Whatever makes you think that?"

Alain undid his cravat in a single, well-executed pull. "Don't play the numbskull with me, Bella. You're not so addlepated not to know he's in love with you. One of these days, he's going to feel encouraged enough to propose. He's bought the horse farm."

"I know."

Alain continued. "What will you do? Driscoll's a good sort, second son to an earl. There's a chance he'll inherit something from his mother's side in the way of a title through a cousinly connection. He loves horses and country living. The two of you get on well and this time you can marry where you like, within reason."

"Enough, Alain," Isabella snapped. "I am in no mood to discuss a hypothetical proposal tonight."

Alain stretched his long legs across the carriage and put his hands behind his head. "Does your waspish mood have anything to do with Tristan's disappearance this evening?"

"Why should it? I am tired. It's been a wearing two weeks thanks to Tristan's penchant for landing himself in the suds and me along with him. Between falling planters and reappearing lightskirts, it's been deuced awkward to find him a wife."

"Deuced is a man's term. You shouldn't use slang."

"Tristan shouldn't provoke me to use it!" Isabella shot back.

"If disappearing with Tristan makes you this peckish, I hope you don't indulge in it often."

It had been on the tip of Isabella's tongue to deny it when she realized the trap. How did Alain know she'd been with Tristan? "I was with Driscoll when Tristan left for his appointment. Shortly after that, I went to the ladies' retiring room. I did *not* disappear with Tristan."

"I beg your pardon then, my mistake." Alain slouched in his seat and closed his eyes. The conversation was over.

Tristan hummed to himself as he unlocked his front door and stepped inside. The sight greeting him in the dimly lit foyer brought an immediate halt to his tune. Vases lay shattered on the floor, broken blooms and stems strewn among the shards of delicate glass. The sight of such wanton destruction inside his own private residence lit a primitive fire in him and he began to roar.

"Sommes! Sommes!" Tristan bellowed for the butler as he strode purposefully through the hall, his shoes crunching on the glass. He reached the front drawing room where the other vases were located and noticed immediately nothing was out of order in that room, but a quick look at the vases revealed what he had suspected: the cards were gone. Someone had taken the bait and there had been a struggle, which explained why the vases were broken in the hall and not in the drawing room. A good thief would make it look as if nothing was out of place. He wouldn't deliberately leave a mess. The longer it took anyone to realize anything was missing, the better the thief's chance of going undetected. Someone must have caught the intruder on his way out.

"My lord, we've had a bit of an accident, as you can see."

The housekeeper, Mrs. Stanton said behind him in the drawing room doorway. "We're all in the kitchen. I came up as
soon as I heard you call."

The usually efficient woman seemed shaken. Tristan
thought perhaps the break-in had been only a short time ago.
"Very well, Mrs. Stanton. Is everyone all right? I'll come
down to the kitchen immediately and talk to all who were
here," Tristan said in his best authoritative tone.

"That wouldn't be proper, my lord. We'll come up
momentarily," she insisted. "Mr. Sommes was hurt in the
altercation. He noticed the burglar first and tried to stop him.
Meg's in the kitchen tending him now."

"I will come with you. No need to stand on propriety tonight, Mrs. Stanton," Tristan said firmly, walking towards
the stairs that led down below Mrs. Stanton, like most who
argued with Tristan, had lost.

The small Gresham household employed a meager staff
of ten: the housekeeper, a groom, a tiger, a downstairs maid,
a tweenie, his valet, a footman, a cook, a cook's helper and
the ever-reliable Sommes around whom everyone hovered
anxiously. Their employer's presence in the servants'
domain caused them an extra amount of anxiety. They
tugged nervously at forelocks and made awkward curtsies
until Mrs. Stanton clapped her hands and instantly settled
them around her long work table.

"Attention, all of you," she instructed sternly. "Keep your
wits together so you can help his lordship understand what
took place here this evening."

Tristan listened with all his keenly honed concentration
for over an hour to each of the different accounts regarding
the theft. As with most situations of this type, there were
disagreements over the facts and varying degrees of accura-
cy when it came to telling the tales. The only facts that
seemed to be certain were that the theft had occurred
around ten o'clock. The thief had entered from the garden-
facing window in the study, made his way to the drawing
room and then into the foyer where Sommes had appre-

hended him. Most telling of all was Sommes's insight that he believed the thief was attempting to leave by the front door.

That was when the fight had taken place. Sommes had tried to stop the intruder. Sommes had landed a few blows of his own, but clearly had taken the brunt of the fight: a black eye and bruised jaw. Whoever had hit him had been a bruising pugilist. In the skirmish, vases had been knocked over and in the end as the man darted away, he'd slowed Sommes's progress by shattering the remaining vases in his path.

Sommes was the only one who had got a good look at the intruder, but the physical description offered little help. The man had been tall, slender in build but strongly made from the impact of his punches. He had dressed all in black and had covered his hair with a dark kerchief and another wrapped around his face, leaving only his eyes visible. Sommes speculated the hair peeking from beneath the coverings was blondish, but in the dark it was impossible to be sure.

Tristan drummed his fingers on the table. "Anything else, Sommes?"

"He moved gracefully, as if he might be a fine dancer, my lord," Sommes offered hesitantly. "He had a way about him that made me think he might be an aristocrat."

Tristan nodded. Halsey had already told him that much. It bothered him that the man knew precisely where to look for the vases. The man had entered by the study window and yet hadn't stopped to look through the study for other secrets or telling correspondence. He had gone straight to the vases, taken the cards and tried to leave by the front door. Tristan supposed that made sense. Going back to the study required backtracking into the depths of the house and posed more chance of being discovered. There were risks, too with going out the front door. Perhaps no one on the inside would notice, but someone on the outside may be suspicious of such a character exiting the home of a wealthy nobleman. Unless that person was someone others would take no notice of if they were passing by because they would expect to see him at Tristan's residence.

"Sommes, tell me again how this man was dressed." Tristan asked, his mind whirling with suppositions. "Do you remember what style or cut? Could you tell the fabric?"

Sommes looked thoughtful. "Evening clothes, I am fairly certain, my lord. The jacket was cut nicely, I think, well-tailored. It didn't rip when we brawled. Good material, maybe a fine wool."

A cold clenching took up residence in Tristan's stomach. All the intruder would have to do was simply take off the obscuring kerchief and blend into the evening with other party goers. "Is there anything else?" Tristan asked.

Somme spoke up again. "I am sorry about the cards. I don't know why someone would want them, but they're obviously of value. Thank goodness the intruder didn't get them all."

Tristan startled at that. "What do you mean he didn't get them all?"

"Why, your friend, Baron Wickham was here earlier tonight. He asked if you were at home but you'd already left for the club. He took a few of the cards with him. I didn't think you'd mind seeing as how the two of you are fast friends."

Tristan rose, not sure what to make of the revelation. Had Alain taken the cards as a sampling and then decided they were legitimate and come back for the rest, knowing he was gone? He didn't like the confirmation that the burglar was tall and blond, dressed in evening clothes. The description could fit Alain. Although, he reminded himself sternly, the description could fit any number of men. The fly in the ointment was Alain's appearance at the town house that night and the fact that Alain had shown marked interest in the cards earlier.

Tristan took a bag of coins from his jacket. "Mrs. Stanton, see that everyone is compensated for their discomfort this evening. I thank you all. I think it is time we were abed." He nodded at his valet. "Jackson, I will not require your services tonight. Get yourself some rest."

Tristan sat up in his chamber, filled with restlessness. He needed to sleep. Tomorrow would be a busy day. He would have to report discreetly to Halsey that the bait had been taken. He had to make the rounds to the clubs and see if anyone was sporting a facer. The description of the burglar had unnerved him. Although the description fit Alain more than adequately, he cautioned himself not to overreact. The description was minimal at best and could be used to describe a hundred other men of the *ton,* even the impeccable Lord Driscoll.

Well, he knew without a doubt the intruder wasn't Lord Driscoll since he'd returned from his liaison and spied Isabella and Driscoll in a cozy conversation. The sight of the two of them had infuriated him. Mostly, Driscoll infuriated him because Driscoll was so likeable. There was nothing wrong with him other than his being besotted with Isabella. A gut wrenching thought crossed Tristan's mind. Did Isabella return Driscoll's affections?

Tristan reached up to his neck and pulled his hair loose of the cord that held it back. He massaged his neck with his right hand and flexed his left, exercising away some of the stiffness.

Tristan walked to the window casement and looked out on the deceptively peaceful city. Cities were never peaceful. Evil roiled about at all hours of the day. He knew. He'd been a part of it. All for a good cause, of course. Tristan snorted at the naïve argument he'd made to himself countless times on other evenings just like this. When had things become so complicated? Halsey had been wrong when he'd said this last assignment would be simple.

There was nothing simple about it. His best friend was a potential suspect, an unknown woman was parading about as his secret admirer, Beatrix's presence complicated matters with Isabella, his home had been violated and the longer he took to catch the double agent, the greater his chances were that Isabella would be won by another. And why not? Why would she prefer a man who could not tell her the truth and exposed her to danger when she could have the imminently suitable Lord Driscoll?

Suddenly, Tristan laughed out loud. "Buck up, Gresham, you nodcock. Isabella doesn't know you love her." Well, that was one thing he could remedy. He'd have to tell her and soon despite his earlier resolution to put his declaration aside until the assignment was complete. He saw now that he could not risk waiting further.

Isabella sat amidst her guests at her late morning at-home, hard pressed to keep her thoughts on the conversation swirling about her. Thankfully, most of her guests were regulars and knew each other well. Today, her guests' inclinations to seek each other out for good company was a boon. Her mind was still overwhelmed by the events of the last evening. Between Avery's near proposal and Tristan's outrageous behavior, it was little wonder she didn't detect the arrival of her latest guest.

George Condon, fourth earl of Middleton, stood in the doorway of the salon and surveyed the room, his keen shooter's eye serving him well in quartering the room and taking notice of who was present. He was not disappointed in the attendance. As a fellow horse lover and general sportsman, he'd guessed correctly. Lady Westbrooke had drawn to her all the riders and horse breeders of any account who needed an oasis in the dead of winter where they could talk at will about their mutual passion. Men as well as women peopled the event, as he'd hoped. They were the perfect audience for his topic of discussion, the nearly wild stallion, Hellion, he was scheduled to auction at Tattersall's.

He'd brought Hellion up to town in the hopes of instigating a bidding war by showing him off. It was a potentially costly gamble. Keeping any horse in town was a pricey luxury and Hellion was an expense he could ill afford these days. But he understood implicitly that appearances were everything. He'd never get top dollar for Hellion if anyone guessed the true dire nature of his financial circumstances.

If he could last the month none of it would matter. In a few weeks, his one outstanding business transaction would be complete. His funds would be flush again and no one would be the wiser to his deceits. Unfortunately, Hellion would have to be sacrificed in the meantime to plump his pockets. Hellion was a magnificent animal but there would be other horses, finer horses, available to him later. He could not dwell on his temporary monetary set backs.

He had come to Lady Westbrooke's with a mission in mind. It was time to go to work, starting with his hostess. George Condon tugged on the lapels of his olive morning coat, knowing that he looked his best. His best was still quite handsome at forty-two, his blond hair hid well any signs of gray and his sporting appetites had kept his figure trim. Confidently, he strode over to greet his hostess.

"Lady Westbrooke, you have achieved quite a turn out," he complimented suavely, taking her hand.

She smiled blandly. "Where else are such like-minded people to gather and wait out the days until spring?"

"My thoughts, precisely," he replied easily, helping himself to the recently vacated chair next to her.

"I hear you've brought Hellion up." The marchioness's eyes sparkled in anticipation, like a child waiting for a treat.

"I thought it would give my more interested buyers a chance to look him over before the auction," Middleton offered mildly, as if he hadn't anything on the line with the upcoming sale.

They spoke about horses and then Middleton stood up, preparing to mingle. He introduced his second point of business as benignly as the first, casting a casual glance around the room. "I don't see Gresham. Is he expected?"

"Gresham is his own man," Lady Westbrooke replied vaguely in a tone that surprised him since he knew she and her brother had been friends with the man for years.

It was an unfortunate piece of luck that Gresham was absent and that Lady Westbrooke did not know his plans. When she offered nothing more regarding Gresham, Middleton took his leave. "I shall just have to track him down then. Again, thank you for your invitation."

Isabella watched Middleton retreat into the crowd. She knew why he was here. It was a prime place to promote his stallion. She scanned the room, doing an efficient check to make sure her guests had all they needed. She caught her butler, Regis's, eye and subtly beckoned him. "What is it, Regis?"

"This note arrived for you, my lady." He held out the silver salver and presented Isabella with an ivory envelope.

"Thank you, Regis. Wait a moment for my reply." Isabella turned the envelope over and recognized the seal as Tristan's. A burst of excitement sped through her and her fingers trembled as she broke the seal. She was giddy like a schoolroom miss and for no good reason. His note had nothing to do with the encounter in the conservatory, how could it? She read the polite but short note twice. Tristan wanted her to drive with him in the park that afternoon at three o'clock. He had something important to tell her. She thought of Driscoll's "important news" the prior evening. She didn't know how much more "important news" she could take.

"What shall I tell the gentleman?" Regis inquired after it was clear she was finished reading the note.

"Tell him yes." Whatever Tristan wanted to share with her, she did not have to worry about it being a marriage proposal. But instead of feeling relieved, Isabella felt strangely disconsolate.

Chapter Nine

"What gorgeous horses! They look like prime goers. Where did you get this rig?" Isabella exclaimed with a mixture of delight and trepidation as Tristan handed her up into the canary-colored high-perch phaeton pulled by a pair of matching grays ten minutes after three o'clock. Whatever anxiety she'd felt about encountering Tristan after the disturbing meeting in the conservatory fled in the wake of her appreciation for the rig and horses waiting outside her town house.

"I have it on loan from a carriage manufacturer who sent it on the train from Manchester. I am thinking of buying it. Such a fancy rig isn't much use to me in the country, but I will need something to drive around town whenever I come up." Tristan saw her settled in the high leather seat and bounded around to the left side, springing into the space next to her in one impressive movement. "What do you think of it, Bella?" he asked, excitement evident in his voice as he clucked to the horses.

"It's very high up," Isabella said uneasily once she realized the precarious nature of the bench seat. She pulled her Lyons' shawl about her as Tristan turned the horses into traffic. "I will need some time to get used to it."

"Ha, Isabella, you're full of contradictions!" Tristan laughed. "You think nothing of riding hell bent for leather but find yourself squeamish over a carriage ride."

Isabella let go of her grip on the small rail next to her seat long enough to playfully swat at Tristan. "That's entirely different. When I am on a horse, I am in complete control. The horse and I know exactly what to expect from each other."

Tristan expertly tooled the phaeton towards the entrance to Hyde Park. "Well, you know what to expect from me. I am as tame to your hand as any horse in your stable. I would not let you fall, Bella, if that's what you fear."

Isabella felt his eyes on her briefly as he spoke the last words and she heard the wealth of unspoken meaning in the words. There was much she wanted explained in that last statement but the park at that crowded hour was no time to broach such an intimate subject. Instead, she steered the conversation back to the phaeton. "I own there is an excellent view from up here. Is the carriage why you're in such good spirits? I assume it must be the important news you mentioned in your note this morning."

"No, the carriage is only part of it. I knew you'd like seeing it and trying out the horses, but it isn't why I requested your company. I am in high spirits because I have made some decisions. I want to share them with you, with your permission, of course. I thought we'd drive down by Rutledge's Pond and shake off some of this crowd."

They were silent as Tristan drove them deeper into the park where the gatherings of people were thinner. In a few weeks, the park would be full of the *beau monde,* but with March barely underway, it was still manageable to find some privacy. Occasionally, Isabella would wave to an acquaintance or exchange smiles with those they passed in carriages pulled to the verge to visit with others. Isabella was glad for the silence and for the relatively few social niceties she was expected to perform as they drove. She was busy pondering what decisions Tristan might have made. The decision she feared most was that he had somehow settled on a bride.

"Here we are," Tristan exclaimed, throwing his reins to his young tiger that ran to hold the horses' heads. He came around to Isabella's side and swung her down. In an easy motion that belied their years of friendship, he tucked her arm through his.

Isabella laughed up at him. "I have not seen you in such good spirits since you've returned home. I am glad for it, although I am excessively curious for the reason."

Tristan patted her hand. "Come down to the pond with me, Bella, so we can talk without being overheard. I have much to tell you. Truth be told, I am amazed myself that I am in such high spirits after what happened last night."

Last night? Warnings sounded in her head. Did he know? Had he guessed so easily? Cautiously, Isabella ventured her question. "What happened last night?"

"I returned home to find that I'd received a nasty visit from a burglar."

"How awful, was anything taken? Was anyone hurt?" Questions flowed in a torrent from Isabella. Impulsively, she pressed his sleeve. "Tristan, you weren't harmed were you?"

"A few small things of interest to only the burglar were taken, Bella. Nothing was damaged beyond a few shattered vases. My butler sports a bruised face but all is well. The good that came out of the robbery is that I spent the night thinking. I am a man of action and I've done little of that since my return. I have made myself a target and I mean to put a stop to it. I am home to stay. It is time I start acting like it."

Isabella looked at him expectantly. The energy coursing through Tristan was contagious. It was powerful enough to momentarily sweep away her doubts about the man she'd seen in him at the winter fete. She wanted to be part of whatever it was he proposed. He had made her feel this way countless times in their youth. "I will do whatever you need done, although I am sure I'll regret it. I seem to recall several past instances when you and Alain convinced me to do some absolutely insane things that landed me in near-run situations."

Tristan stopped them at the pond's edge and turned to face her. "Bella, don't pretend you've given up taking risks. Remember, I heard you take the Valentine's wager with Alain to see me wed by June and I know you are set on acquiring Middleton's wild stallion. Assisting me in taking charge of my new life is a minimal risk for you when all is said and done."

"So far, you've managed to land me in the middle of your little scandal about a murky past. I'd hardly call that minimal, Tristan," Isabella reminded him.

He laughed it off. "That will pass once the Season is in full swing. Within a month, no one will care about Viscount Gresham's outlandish entertainments on the Continent over a year ago. I am surprised they cared at all. No one would have thought twice if Beatrix hadn't made such a display."

"Parents will care when you decide to marry their daughter," Isabella chided. "By your own admission, you want to marry quickly. If I am successful, and I will be, you'll be leg-shackled by June. That's three short months away. People will remember the rumors."

Tristan's dark eyes turned thoughtful. "It is good to talk with you like this, Bella. I missed our quiet walks and conversations while I was away." He ran his hands up and down Isabella's arms in a languorous motion. "Did you know, while I was gone I'd talk to you in my head? When things were at their worst, I'd lie in my bed at night and talk them all through with you. I could close my eyes and imagine we were at Summer Hill, at your father's place, walking the meadows."

"Those days were long ago," Isabella hedged. The conversation was taking a decidedly uncomfortable turn. She shivered in spite of the warmth of his hands on her arms. Who was this enigma who had kissed her with the expertise

of a rogue last night and now stood before her in the guise
of her one-time best friend? When he was like this, she had
no doubt who he was. But the rumors and the first hand
demonstration were sharp reminders that Tristan was not all
he seemed. A brown wren chirped from its nest, its warble
piercing the quietness around them, reminding Isabella of
the prolonged silence which had sprung up between them.
Tristan was looking at her intently, apparently not as
unnerved as she by the dearth of conversation between
them.

"You still haven't told me about the decisions you've
made," Isabella prompted.

Tristan smiled softly. "So I haven't. I want to give a house
party at The Meadows. I want you to act as hostess. You'll
know who to invite and what kinds of suitable entertainments to offer. I want to do it at the end of March. I know it
is short notice, only a few weeks. I haven't seen the place in
years but I believe it is in good shape. Say you'll do it."

A house party? All this intimacy for a house party? It took
Isabella a moment to adjust her thoughts. What a silly goose
she was. What had she thought he was going to say?

She heard herself agreeing. "Of course I'll do it, Tristan.
But tell me why you want to give a house party?"

"Because I am a man of action, as I said earlier. I have
made myself a target by waiting for Society to introduce
itself to me. Here in London, I must rely on the hostesses'
invitations. My house party will be my chance to introduce
myself to Society. At my place in the country, I am in
charge." He winked at Isabella. "I believe you know a thing
or two about the desirable nature of being in control."

"Touché! A gentleman does not remind a lady of her
brash words." Isabella paced in the grass, her long fingers
tapping her chin while she thought out loud. "At any rate, it's
a splendid idea. People will be clamoring for invitations
simply to meet you. Everyone will want to have a chance to
confirm for themselves the truth of the conjectures being
made about you. We'll keep the party short, just four days."

Tristan fell into step beside her. "I definitely want a ball one evening."

"That's ambitious. A ball requires at least two hundred people in attendance or it will be termed a dismal failure. We can have dancing, Tristan. Perhaps something more informal would be better."

"No," Tristan insisted. "I want a ball. We can invite the neighbors. We can invite the entire village if that's what it takes to make up the numbers." Determination fired his countenance. Isabella thought he looked magnificent in his buff trousers and fitted green jacket as he stood there arguing for his ball. No wonder Napoleon had been defeated. Tristan would brook no dispute from anyone.

"What is your attachment to having a ball?" Isabella queried, "Such an adamant demand must have a motive behind it."

Tristan grabbed her hands and looked at her in all seriousness. "That's the second decision I made last night. I mean to announce my betrothal."

Isabella barely suppressed a gasp. She was entirely unsure what emotion to display. Surprise? Happiness? "Who is she, Tristan?" Her voice shook.

"It's you." Tristan sank to a knee in the damp reeds by the pond, capturing her gloved hands in his. "Marry me, Isabella."

"Tristan, you can't be serious." She tried to pull her hands away but Tristan held them resolutely.

"I confess I have not done much proposing, Bella, but I assure you I am in earnest. It is the only match that makes sense." He rose and brushed at his breeches. "You're obligated to accept since I've muddied my pants on your behalf. It would be bad form not to." He jested weakly.

Isabella heard the desperation in his voice. "I am sorry, Tristan. I have handled this badly. I am overwhelmed. I did not expect this."

"You did not? How could you not know how I feel about you? How I have always felt about you?" Tristan argued.

"All those years away, my love did not falter. I left England because I could not stay knowing you were the wife of another. My feelings for you have not changed since the day we parted." Tristan poured out his confession in a torrent of heartfelt passion. His face paled suddenly. "Isabella, my feelings have not changed. Have yours? Is it Driscoll?" There was panic in his voice.

If the situation had not seemed so absurd, Isabella would have found Tristan's earnest school boy nature highly amusing compared to the worldly performance he'd given in the conservatory.

"Avery Driscoll has no claim on my affections beyond friendship."

"Is there someone else?"

"No. There's no one else."

"Then why do you resist?" Tristan asked, utterly perplexed.

"Tristan, we do not know each other. We are not the same people we were years ago. I behaved impetuously the day I asked you to marry me. I should not have done it. I have regretted it a thousand times over. You went away because of me. You could have been killed. I am not that same impulsive girl." It was the kindest way she could think of to voice her objections to the match, although her heart still pounded rapidly at the prospect. Tristan had proposed!

His face became thunderous. Isabella knew he'd understood the message. "You say you are not the same impulsive girl. Does that mean you believe I am not the same honorable man you once knew?"

She hated herself for the pain she caused him. "You go too far, Tristan. It means only that I don't know you anymore." She held up her gloved hand in a stalling motion when he made to protest. "You've come home with your hand scarred to near destruction and you won't tell me why. Rumors, which you will neither deny nor confirm, abound about the nature of your military service. The vulgar Beatrix Smallwood's association with you does you no credit. A secret admirer lurks in the background, sending you flowers.

Your home is burglarized and someone tosses a planter off a roof at you."

Isabella gave an unladylike bark. "You say you're tired of not taking action, but I think that's plenty of action for the mere three weeks you've been home." Isabella broke off her tirade. She felt a bit sheepish in the wake of her vented spleen. Only Tristan roused her temper like this. She hadn't had such a row in ages. Tristan's eyes were uncharacteristically misty. Were those tears he fought so vainly to hide? Unable to look at his achingly handsome face any longer, she stared at the ground, suddenly engrossed in the half boots that poked out from beneath her carriage dress. When Tristan spoke, she'd get the tongue lashing she deserved for speaking too freely. Then, he'd recant his proposal, glad that he'd escaped marrying such a forthright shrew.

"You've always had a knack for helping me see issues clearly." Tristan spoke quietly.

Isabella hazarded an upward glance. She was surprised to notice that he too had developed a penchant for gazing at his boots. "Don't be angry with me for stating the truth."

"That's where you're wrong, my dear." Tristan stripped off his gloves and tucked them into a coat pocket. "This is the truth." He cupped her face between his bare hands and gently pulled her to him.

His kiss was all tenderness and longing when their lips met. There was none of the force or manipulation that had been present in the conservatory. This kiss tasted of sweet honesty. Isabella sighed beneath his mouth. She whispered his name when they parted. "Tristan."

"I want to do more than kiss you, Isabella. But I would have marriage between us first. Say you'll reconsider."

"I don't recall actually refusing you," Isabella said somewhat saucily as she recovered her breath.

Tristan growled low in his throat. "Vixen! Perhaps you need more persuading?" He bent to kiss her again. Isabella laid a hand against his chest, calling a halt to his actions. A fleeting recollection of another woman who had made such a gesture flashed through his mind before being discarded.

"Tristan, one sweet kiss does not change what lies between us. Persuade me by answering my questions."

Tristan nodded. He captured the hand that lay against his chest in his own. "I ask for your trust and your time. I will tell you all when I can but that time is not yet."

"Then I must tell you that I will hold your marriage offer in trust against that day," Isabella replied with all the strength she could muster. She wanted nothing more than to accept Tristan's proposal. She was not foolish. She knew herself well enough to know that she wanted to marry the Tristan of her youth. She did not know the man who stood before her well enough yet to entrust him with her heart.

"Is that the best you can do, Isabella?" Tristan whispered.

"Yes, Tristan, it is the best I can do. I think you should take me home now."

The drive home was accomplished in silence, their moods decidedly more somber than when they had set out two hours ago. When they arrived at Westbrooke House, Tristan handed Isabella down from the high seat and bowed politely over her hand. "Shall I see you and Alain tonight at the Fillmore soiree?"

"I have not yet made up my mind if I'll attend. Alain left a note earlier this morning saying that he'd be at The Refuge for a few days checking on some of his pet projects."

"Then I shall hope for the best. Until tonight," Tristan said gallantly before climbing up and clucking to his horses. It was too bad Alain would not be present, he thought as he steered the rig towards home. He would have liked to have cleared Alain of any suspicions once and for all by seeing that Alain did not bear the marks of a scuffle with Sommes on his face. By the time Alain returned to town, a black eye would have faded. His assignment was getting deuced complicated.

It was complicated further when a note arrived at the

town house an hour later from the secret admirer. She wanted to meet again that evening at the Fillmore soiree.

Isabella knew the Fillmore's house well. There were not many secret places to meet, so she had sent word to Gresham that his admirer would await him in the garden near the cupid fountain. She drew her heavy velvet cloak about her as she took a seat on the stone bench. Already she was chilled. Perhaps it had been foolish to meet in the freezing, deserted garden. The cupid fountain dripped icicles and she shivered despite the warmth of her cloak. There had been no other choice. The interior of the house was not suited for a clandestine meeting. No one would be in the garden and the garden was dark, two factors which doubly recommended the place. The only light touching it came from the drawing room where everyone was gathered. She could stand in plain sight on one of the paths and no one would be able to see her.

Isabella mentally added unsafe to her list of adjectives describing her choice of meeting places. If anyone intent on foul deeds was prowling the grounds they'd have no trouble taking her at unawares and going unnoticed by the throng of people one hundred yards away.

She hadn't wanted to play the admirer again. The first meeting had shaken her sensibilities greatly. A large part of her wanted to live in ignorant bliss about Tristan's past. After his proposal today, that was no longer an option. If she was going to bind her life to his in marriage, she had to know the truth. She would be terribly crushed if she walked into such a relationship without her eyes wide open. Tonight, she would push him for the vital answers she needed.

Isabella had thought her senses were keenly alert in the darkness but she didn't hear Tristan approach until he was behind her, so close his breath felt warm against her neck in startling contrast to the cold. She jumped and bit back a startled scream.

"*Ma cherie*, that should teach you a lesson for choosing

such shadowy places to meet," he said in a low tone that was at once both sinister and seductive. "I am surprised to see you here so early. Have you been waiting long?" He took her gloved hands in his and sat beside her on the stone bench. "Your hands are chilled. Silk gloves are no protection against the cold," he scolded gently, chafing them in his own warm hands. Isabella wondered if he would notice the gloves were new since he now possessed the mate to her other set.

"Are you not cold?" Isabella asked, noting that he wore only his dark evening coat. She knew from personal association that he was a veritable furnace, his body usually generating an inhuman amount of heat, but even against the wintry chill of the evening he must feel some discomfort.

He shook his head. "How can I be cold when I have such a companion to warm me with her presence? To what ends shall we put this meeting of ours?"

Isabella jerked her hand from his, immediately feeling the loss of his heat, and stood up. "Save your flattery and glib tongue for the young debutantes," she snapped.

Tristan laughed softly in the darkness and stretched out his long legs. "I propose a game. Are you familiar with the story of Rumpelstiltskin?"

"The children's tale? Yes," Isabella replied warily.

"The miller's daughter does not keep her promise and Rumpelstiltskin allows her to forego her obligation to him if she can guess his name in three evenings." Tristan continued. "A variation of the same game would suit us well. I had hoped you'd reveal yourself to me, so we would be done with black cloaks and veils, but I see that we are not. If I guess your name, you must confess all." He was leaning close to her, the smell of peppermints on his breath. "You may ask three questions of me tonight. For every question you ask, I get to make a guess as to your name."

Isabella gave a haughty laugh that suggested more confidence than she felt. "What do I get if you fail?"

Tristan reached into a pocket and pulled out a long silk

glove with pearl buttons. "This. I believe you left it at our last encounter."

Isabella instinctively reached for it but he held it out of her grasp and laughed. "I will most likely fail in my task. Three names are not that many. The glove shall be yours soon enough. Come and sit with me then and let us discuss ourselves. Despite your insinuation at our last meeting that we are not strangers, I find it quite disconcerting that you know me and I do not know anything of you. I shall bide my time. Ladies first, ask your question."

What was it Amy had advised when this charade had begun? Get a man to talk about himself? Isabella put some distance between them on the bench. "Tell me about your work in France. It sounds very dangerous."

Tristan folded his arms, his posture alert. "I was a reconnaissance officer. I scouted out the enemy before battles in order to determine their strength, size and location."

That was it? That's all he had to say? Isabella's shoulders sagged in disappointed. Didn't he know this was his chance to impress her with his military career? He was supposed to have more to say than that.

Daringly, Isabella leaned forward and traced his cheek with a soft silk clad finger. "You did that for seven years. You must have been quite good at it. Were you ever in jeopardy? You must have exciting stories to tell."

"Is that your second question?"

"I expected to have you say more than two sentences. It hardly seems fair to get so little for one's question," Isabella complained.

"Our rules didn't suggest that I had to give my life's history in order for the answer to be complete," Tristan countered smoothly. "Now, here's my first guess: Cynthia."

Isabella let out a breath. "No. Second question, who is Beatrix Smallwood to you?"

"Are we jealous, *ma cherie*?" Tristan tut-tutted.

"Absolutely not, I am merely curious as to the nature of my rival."

"Mrs. Smallwood is an old acquaintance. We have our Continental experiences in common. Perhaps she believes there is more between us than there is. Your shoulders sag. I see you're disappointed in my answer. Would you like it better if I told you a sordid tale about our history together?"

"Of course not!" Isabella replied hotly. "Why would you think that?"

"I imagine you have your own expectations regarding me. I'd hate to not live up to the incredibly low opinions currently circulating about my war record."

"Are those opinions the truth then?"

"Is that your third question?"

"Yes," Isabella said crossly. "I am capable of counting."

"Then you'll appreciate the fact that I allowed you an extra question. Don't forget I have two guesses owing to me." Tristan was smug. "As to an answer, I can only say that most lies spring from some nugget of truth."

"What kind of answer is that?"

"My answer. Now—" Tristan didn't get any further.

"Oh, I say! I am sorry I didn't know anyone was there." A voice broke into their trysting place. The voice sounded far too contrived to convince Isabella the intruder had been startled by his immediate discovery. This voice belonged to someone who'd been watching, at least briefly, and it sounded familiar.

How much had the intruder heard? She wasn't worried as much for herself as she was for Tristan. The intruder could tell nothing of her identity under her wraps but perhaps he would make something ludicrous out of Tristan's veiled statements. To his credit, Tristan rose from the bench and stepped in front of her, effectively blocking the intruder's view of her. He strode forward and clapped the man on the shoulder with great bonhomie and steered him back towards the drawing room. Isabella could hear traces of their conversation as they walked away.

"Gresham, it is you, you old devil! I couldn't see well enough in the darkness but I am not surprised. I came outside for some fresh air, but instead I run across your little liaison with your secret admirer. Lud, you have all the luck. Do you know who it is yet?" The intruder rambled on. "You're a bold one, Gresham, carrying on like that and not even knowing who's under the covers."

"Does it really matter, Middleton?" Tristan said rather coldly.

Male laughter floated back to Isabella. "I suppose it doesn't, Gresham. They're all the same in the dark."

Isabella grabbed a handful of rocks and threw them at the fence in frustration. Of all the gall! How could Tristan hoax her like this? Truly, he was a rogue of the first water to play with her the way he had at the pond. It was utterly vile to toy with her affections by pretending such sincerity as he had shown this afternoon, and then jaunt off to meet with an anonymous woman of purportedly brazen character hours later. It was entirely unconscionable. She couldn't imagine what would compel such behavior. Unless, she had it backwards and for some unfathomable reason the show he'd put on tonight was the lie. If that was the case, she was no closer to knowing.

Chapter Ten

Tristan gave the amber liquid in his snifter a distracted swirl. His feet rested on the fireplace fender. He registered the long case clock chiming two hours after midnight in the hall. He should try and sleep but his mind was not tired. He had come home early from the Fillmore soiree, disconsolate and confused. After he had walked Middleton back inside he had returned to the bench and found it empty. He had suspected he would. The admirer was gone as was any chance to confirm her identity.

Several things bothered him about the admirer. Instinctively, he felt he should know her. She had mannerisms and other characteristics that he knew.

In his line of work, he'd learned to rely on all of his senses. Methodically, he dissected the information he knew about her according to each sense. She was taller than most women. Beneath her voluminous cloak, she seemed to have a slender, athletic frame. But to rely on sight alone exposed one to lies. Anyone could disguise his or her physical appearance. Her heavy veil had concealed a good look at her eyes and totally distorted the proportions of her face. Her voice was husky and deliberately pitched low. The attempt to match the voice did not fool Tristan in the least. Her true voice would sound much different. There weren't many clues in the sight and sound of her. The chinks in her disguise were in her touch and her smell.

Touch conveyed all manner of secrets people wanted to keep hidden. He hadn't wanted to act the forward rogue and practice seduction on her, but it was a surefire way to know what her touch revealed. She had wanted to appear sophisticated and worldly to him. Her touches would have been bold if she'd been comfortable carrying them off. She was not. When things were getting interesting, she'd stopped his hand and push against his chest, just as Isabella had in the park.

His thoughts drifted to Isabella, testing the similarities. The names he'd guessed were the names of two women present at the Fillmore soiree who seemed most likely to engage in borderline behavior, but they had not necessarily fit the description he had concocted of the secret admirer. Isabella was tall and moved with an athletic agility. Isabella had used the same gesture. Isabella lacked the true worldliness she affected so well. Isabella smelled of roses. That was the clincher.

People could often manufacture any nature of visual disguise, but smell was more difficult to overcome, usually because people overlooked the reality that they carried with them a unique smell that marked them as individuals. One of the many sobriquets Tristan had acquired on the Continent in quieter, darker circles was "bloodhound." The first question he asked about the people he tracked was "what do they smell like?" People might layer their scents, cover them up with other smells, but they couldn't subdue them entirely. The admirer had smelled of vanilla under which was the scent of roses. Isabella preferred to bath in rosewater, it was one of her signature trademarks.

He wanted to reject the notion that Isabella was the unwanted admirer, but how could he deny the facts? Why would Isabella insinuate herself into such a precarious situation? The motivations and their consequences were sinister. Perhaps she was looking for answers to his past? She had indicated on several occasions that those answers were important to her. If so, it was no wonder she'd shown such hesitation over his proposal today. She was aware of his duality but not the cause for it. She wanted to know which Tristan Moreland was real; the one who spoke of friendship and honesty in the afternoons or the one who met with outrageous women in dark rooms at parties. His heart lurched at the thought she might pick the wrong identity to believe.

That was the least of his worries. The other motivation was more severe. Perhaps she posed as the admirer to protect Alain. He had been with her at the Briarton winter ball at the same time his town house had been broken into. Had she been the decoy to ensure that he'd be occupied while Alain slipped away? He definitely remembered Alain being absent after his arrival at the ball. Briarton House was only a few blocks from his mansion. It wasn't unseemly that Alain had slipped out a back garden gate and covered the distance in a few short minutes.

The devil fly away with it! Tristan cursed, swallowing the remaining brandy in his snifter. He was tired of secrets and conjecture. The sooner he got Isabella to the country, the sooner he could have his answers. The Meadows was only fifteen miles outside of London, a half day's trip on good roads. If they left by early afternoon, they could make the estate by evening. He would press her on an early departure tomorrow morning.

Isabella stared blankly at the empty stationery in front of her. She'd been trying in vain to compose a simple letter to a friend in Devon for the past hour. She couldn't get past the salutation without her thoughts being taken up by the events of the prior evening.

She had been a fool for thinking she could control Tristan. At the Fillmore's he had done as exactly as he wished and she had put up no opposition to participating in his decadent games. What did that make her? She pressed her fingers to her temples, refusing to contemplate the names that sprang to mind. What would she have done if he'd kissed her again as he had in the conservatory? Worse, what would she have done if he'd guessed her name?

Amy had been right. This game of secret admirer was too dangerous. She wondered if Amy had anticipated this type of danger. She desperately wanted to talk to someone, to lay her troubles on other shoulders, but this was one thing that could not be shared. She was in this alone. She could not tell Amy about the ravaging kiss they'd shared or that she hadn't found it distasteful.

Everything about Tristan was as fascinating to her now as it had been in the throes of her youthful infatuation for him. With Tristan, the most mundane activity became extraordinary. She had not experienced such a phenomenon with anyone else, not even Westbrooke, who was all that a good husband should have been. Isabella acknowledged that Westbrooke had been a kind and doting husband to his young wife. She had told herself during the years of her marriage that the lack of affection beyond mutual respect was due to the disparity in their ages, but it was the same lack of deep fondness she felt for Avery Driscoll, a man who was her age, handsome and intelligent. Her long-harbored notions had ripened to fruition with Driscoll's courtship and Tristan's return. Tristan, with his sleek dark mane and soulful eyes, had ruined her for other men.

She gave up on the letter and penned a quick note to Amy. Maybe some shopping would help clear her mind.

"How are events progressing with your ill-begotten adventure?" Lady Briarton inquired wryly as she and Isabella strolled down Bond Street, arm in arm. Amy had accepted Isabella's invitation to shop with alacrity. In less than the space of an hour, Isabella had met her friend in front of her favorite milliner's.

"I think the game is progressing," Isabella said resolutely, not sure how to ask her friend for pointers on advancing the game. She couldn't afford to tip her hand or Amy would have the entire sordid story out of her. She wasn't ready for that. Her emotions were still in a state of confusion this morning. She wasn't certain she understood all the twists and turns involved in the convoluted plot, let alone be able to explain them to another.

"Don't be a gudgeon, Isabella. You know such a vague response won't fadge with me. I want details. What have you learned?" Amy nudged her friend, pointing to a bow-fronted window showcasing dress materials. "Let's turn in there. That striped poplin is just the thing!"

The bell jangled as they stepped inside the draper's, thankfully diverting Amy's attention momentarily. She returned to the topic while fingering the ells of poplin brought out by the shopkeeper. "You've been far too close-mouthed since the ball for me to believe that nothing exceptional has happened and yet everything is going smoothly. I deserve some details, at least. After all, I let you practice your deceit in my house." Amy reminded her in a teasing tone.

Isabella sighed heavily. "I think the game has reached a plateau. I will learn nothing more unless I escalate the stakes."

"You will not consider it!" Amy whispered in outrage. "You've learned all you can, Isabella. If you have to escalate the stakes than he is most definitely a rake and the rumors are well warranted."

"That's the problem. I am not exactly sure that the way he behaves with the secret admirer is the truth at all. He's so very different, more like his old self, when we're together during the day." Isabella winced. She'd said too much. Amy's sly look confirmed it.

"I didn't know you'd been seeing him outside of natural social encounters at larger events." Amy looked at the watch attached to her pelisse. "Ah, perfect. Time for luncheon. I think we'd better discuss this development of yours over food. I know a corner café that makes delicious sandwiches not far from here."

Amy beckoned to the shopkeeper and quickly arranged for her purchase to be sent to Briarton House. Then she led a wary Isabella to the café. The two women settled themselves at a small table near the window and ordered sandwiches and tea.

When the sandwiches arrived, Isabella tried a diversionary tactic. "These are delicious. I can't believe I didn't know about this place."

Amy grinned and waved her finger in scolding. "No, no, no, Bella. You won't distract me from my purpose. We'll talk about sandwiches later."

"Tristan took me driving yesterday."

"In the park? Where everyone could see you?" Amy rubbed her hands together in anticipation.

Isabella tried to pass off the event as commonplace. "It was just to try out his new rig and horses. I am sure if Alain had been home, he'd have asked Alain."

"Men don't ask other men to ride in the park with them in their carriages," Amy pointed out bluntly. "What else happened? What did you talk about?"

"He asked me to come to The Meadows and act as hostess for his house party."

"House party? I haven't heard about it."

"We haven't planned it yet." A familiar voice interrupted her.

"Lord Gresham, how good to see you again." Amy offered her hand, a smile plastered on her face. Isabella felt her face go red. She had been caught talking about him!

"I have had the devil's own time tracking you ladies down. I called at Westbrooke House earlier and must have just missed you. Your butler was kind enough to give me your direction and I tracked you from there." He looked at Amy while he spoke, but Isabella had no doubt the words were for her alone.

"I was unaware we had an appointment. Am I mistaken?" she said coolly, trying to hide her chagrin at his forward manner. Without being asked, Tristan had drawn a third chair up to their table. He made it plain he was not passing by for a moment of chit chat.

"No, we did not have an appointment. However, I was struck by a sudden need to see you." His words were a caress that brought a blush to Isabella's hot cheeks. She bristled at the idea that he could reduce her so easily to the status of an insipid schoolroom miss. Thankfully, he turned the conversation to the table at large.

"Lady Briarton, I am throwing a house party at month's end. Lady Westbrooke has graciously agreed to serve as my hostess since her brother and I are such close friends. I haven't got another female relative to turn to. I had thought going down to The Meadows next week would give us sufficient time to open up the place and lay our plans. However, I have discovered there is an urgent need to go sooner. I hope you will help convince her to depart with me at once this afternoon."

"This afternoon?" Isabella gaped at him. "I couldn't possibly be ready. I need two days at least."

He gave her an indulgent look mixed with gentlemanly naiveté. "Lady Westbrooke, how long could it possibly take to pack a few gowns? You can send the rest by post chaise later. I daresay we could be gone in three quarters of an hour."

Isabella stared at Tristan in horror. His proposition had garnered the attention of the surrounding tables. Whispers were starting behind napkins and painted fans. She was mortified. How dare he ask her to go away with him in a public place? By nightfall, Tristan's latest flaunting of convention would be common knowledge among the *ton*. She felt the pressure of his boot on her foot. She glared at him. He leaned forward.

"Bella, forgive me. I must ask you to come with me at once. I have been followed. Do you see that man across the street? He's followed me since I left my house. My phaeton is parked in an alley out back. I want to get us to safety."

The man Tristan indicated started to cross the street. Isabella gasped. "What shall I do?"

"Pretend you're looking for a ladies retiring area. Go through the kitchen and out the back. My tiger is there with the grays."

"We could take my covered coach," Isabella countered.

"It's too far away. Don't argue with me. Just go."

Isabella's pulse raced with excitement and fear. The man was nearly to the café door, all the incentive she needed to rise and make her way to the kitchen. Tristan lounged carelessly in his chair, looking relaxed in the company of Lady Briarton. She tried to emulate his calm as she wended through the little tables. The door opened, its copper bell tinkling. Isabella didn't need to look back to know the man had entered the café.

At the kitchen door, the crashing of dishware and glass drew her attention back to the front table where she'd recently sat. Her breath caught at the sight of Tristan and the stranger grappling amid the ruins of lunch. Isabella briefly looked for Amy, relieved to see that Amy had wisely scooted anonymously to the side, falling in with the terrified onlookers. Something glinted in the man's hand: a knife. Tristan countered with a long blade of his own, flashing into his right hand from nowhere. Isabella was riveted. Where had he kept such a weapon? Did he carry it at all times? Tristan slashed at the man, but Isabella could see his efforts were aimed at survival, not at killing the man.

Tristan thrust the man aside and upended two more tables to block the man's progress. Swiftly, he came towards Isabella. "I told you to go!" He pushed her fiercely before him through the kitchen and hauled her up into the waiting rig. He vaulted up behind her and cracked the reins, shouting to the grays. They pelted down the narrow lane. Turning out into a quiet side street, Isabella glimpsed a man bursting into the alley, too far away to pursue them further.

She gave up gripping the seat rail and opted for gripping Tristan's firm arm. He drove possessed, weaving in and out of traffic with no intention to stop until he was well away from the city. At last the horses slowed to a trot. The city was behind them.

"So much for packing," Isabella commented dryly when she could breathe evenly again. "Do you mind telling me what is going on?"

"I am being followed. Perhaps the burglar wasn't satisfied with what he took from my home and wishes to perpetrate a crime upon my person."

"Why implicate me?"

"Because I feared this criminal may try to get to me by using you as leverage. You were on the balcony with me the night the planter was thrown. Maybe he worries you might have seen him."

"You're bamming me, Tristan," Isabella said bluntly. "I wish you'd stop it and tell me the truth. The truth had better be worth it. You do realize you propositioned me in public place. This will put paid to any chances you had for making a decent marriage."

"I suppose it also scotches your chances for winning the wager and the horse." Tristan's penitent tone put Isabella on guard. She was ready when the caveat came. "Of course, you can still salvage the wager and marry me yourself."

The absurdity of such a comment after their harrowing dash brought a wide smile to Isabella's mouth. Laughter bubbled up and she gave herself over to it. "Tristan! How can you think of such a thing at a time like this?"

He turned to look at her, the grin on his face as wide as her own. "How can I not? I have thought of little else since the night I kissed you seven years ago."

"Back when you were reckless *and* honorable."

"Oh, Isabella, I still am." He winked once and clucked to the horses. She thought he made the phaeton lurch on purpose just so she'd grab for his arm again, the wicked man.

The road ahead was flat and clear. He gave the horses their heads. "Hold on tight love," he crooned to Isabella. "I'll give you the ride of your life." And Isabella did. There'd be the piper to pay. Tristan Moreland was reckless. But was he still honorable?

Chapter Eleven

T he Meadows was a rambling homey affair of a manor that admirably suited their desire for solace and peace. They arrived at the onset of evening, dusty and tired but in good spirits. They were both pleased to see that the manor had received excellent care from the steward in Tristan's absence. Holland covers carefully blanketed the furniture, but effort had been taken to keep the place dusted and polished.

Delighted to have someone to do for, the housekeeper promised a lite but hot dinner within the hour and set the one regular maid to preparing rooms for the evening. Tristan smiled his thanks and offered to take Isabella for a walk down by the pond.

"The last time we walked down by a pond you proposed marriage," Isabella teased, taking his arm.

"I will do so until you accept," Tristan warned, helping her navigate the uneven ground.

Isabella turned serious. "Let us not talk of such things. Let's enjoy this splendid prospect and the beauty that surrounds us." She gestured widely to indicate the lilac and rose hued sky. "I have not seen such a grand sunset for ages. In London, it is all fog and darkness for months on end. Oh, how I miss this!" Impulsively, she threw her arms around his neck. "Thank you for bringing me!"

Tristan laughed with her, enjoying her abandonment for the moment. "Am I forgiven for dragging you into scandal yet again?"

"For now." Isabella dropped her hands and walked a bit apart from him. "We can't ignore the gossip, although I wish we could." She sighed wistfully. "Life would be much simpler if we could simply be."

"We have the next few days at least," Tristan offered in consolation, coming to stand beside her and take her hand in his.

Isabella looked at him sternly. "We do have that, and it is a gift we must not waste by pretending ignorance is bliss. There are many things we must talk about, Tristan, starting with your little performance in the café this afternoon." She saw the reluctance creep into his face. "I won't ask for more than that tonight," she promised.

Tristan nodded. He gazed out over the pond, thinking about where to begin.

"Does it have something to do with your hand?" Isabella prompted.

Tristan took her offering. "Yes." Unexpectedly, the way seemed clear to him. The burden he carried seemed less. He glanced at the sun to gauge how long he had before it became dark. He wanted to tell Isabella all that he could. If he had to move the conversation to the house, he'd lose his momentum. He had enough time, maybe even an hour. His decision made, Tristan swept off his coat in a gallant manner and spread it on the ground. "Your seat, my lady."

Isabella sat and looked at him expectantly. He stretched out beside her, heedless of the damage grass and dirt might do to his buff breeches and white shirt. His dark hair spilled over his shoulder and he ineffectually pushed it back only to have it fall again.

"Leave it," Isabella whispered patiently when he would have pushed his hair back one more time.

Tristan opened his left hand, exposing the scar. "The man who did this ambushed me a few months back on the docks in Paris. I walked into a trap. There were three men waiting for me. I killed two of them with a sword. The third man was highly skilled with blades of any sort. My own sword had been shattered earlier in the fight. I drew my knife, the one you saw this afternoon. He drew his. We prowled around each other looking for an opening. I had no wish to kill him, but I would do whatever was needed to ensure my escape. He thrust at me several times. I have the scars on my arms and torso to prove how effective he was. I was tiring and he was fresh. He sliced my hand. I think he was playing with me, assuming he'd get another chance to really do some damage.

"He called me by my name although I did not know him. That's when I started to realize just how wrong everything had gone that evening. I had to end it all very soon, so the next chance I got, I stabbed hard. It was enough to send him bleeding into the night. I do not think he has forgiven me for the injury I did him, although we're quite even. He has ruined my hand. Nonetheless, he has followed me to England and seeks me out."

"Why did he ambush you in the first place? What could you have done to earn such displeasure?" Isabella's brow furrowed in contemplation.

Tristan looked grim. "This is the harder part of the story to tell, my love, for I fear it will cost me everything I hold dear, and that is you."

"I would have the truth, Tristan. It cannot be worse than living with the ambiguity which surrounds you now," Isabella encouraged softly.

"He ambushed me because I had foiled the latest attempt to engineer Napoleon's escape." Tristan let the announcement sink into Isabella's thoughts. He anticipated her questions. "I was, or rather, I am an agent provocateur for the Crown. During the war, I was part of a secret group charged with gathering information about the enemy. After the war, there was still need of my services. The British had learned from his first escape that Napoleon would stop at nothing. Months earlier, I infiltrated a circle of people who were secretly devoted to the emperor's cause. They were English but they felt there was more to gain by prolonging the war. When I heard the rumors and found them to be substantiated, I arranged to meet with my English connection and pass on the plans."

Isabella picked up the threads of the story. "But your connection was not there that night."

Tristan nodded his head. "He was dead. His body had been dumped in the Seine. It was dredged up the next morning. He had been stabbed."

"Being in the cavalry was a lie?" Isabella asked, puzzling over the various pieces.

"Not entirely. I was in the cavalry for a few months in Spain. It became apparent I had other talents the Crown could put to better use."

Isabella smiled at that. "Better talents than riding a horse? You're the finest rider I know, Tristan. You must have been the most magnificent man on horseback either country had ever seen." Then she sobered. Tristan could see it all fall into place for her like so many tumblers on a lock. In a moment she had it.

"Oh," she said quietly. "I understand now what Mrs. Smallwood meant about not letting any of the ladies languish. You seduced them for information."

Tristan winced. It sounded so much worse when she said it, boiling it down to the least common denominator. "It wasn't quite as crass as all that, Bella. In most cases, the women seduced me. The Crown merely put me in the path of these women who were either involved in treasonous acts, or their husbands or lovers were."

"Mrs. Smallwood told no lies then?" Isabella surmised. She stood up, brushing her skirts.

Tristan rose immediately. "Bella, let me explain. In many cases it was nothing more than flirting, some kissing in the dark." *Good lord, that came out all wrong.* Tristan cringed under the incredulous stare Bella speared him with. "It was all for king and country!" That sounded even worse. He knew he should stop talking but he couldn't halt the words that flooded from his mouth. A long-held dam had burst.

"What was I to do, Bella? I had a chance to do something useful with my life. What else was there for me? You were married to another and from all reports, enjoying life as Lady Westbrooke. I had to find a way to go on. Serving my king seemed as good a choice as any."

"I was Lady Westbrooke because you told me to be! I married him because you would not have it otherwise. You spoke of honor and loyalty the day I came to you and I believed you!" Isabella shouted.

"What would you have had me do? Whisk you off to the Americas and leave all we knew behind us?"

"You could have asked."

"It would have been pointless. I saw the moment you made your decision. When you heard about your family's finances, you let me go. I could see it in your face. If you had kissed me one last time, Bella, given me some indication there was hope. Instead, you walked out the door to embrace your duty. I did the best I could to embrace mine. One kiss, Bella, and I would have moved heaven and earth for you."

Isabella laughed bitterly. "I long thought I'd sent you to your death. Now, I hear that my worries were unfounded. You were throwing parties and wooing women."

Tristan was defensive for a moment. "I was in plenty of danger, Bella. I still am. Mostly, I am in danger of losing you. I was a covert agent and my last mission was jeopardized. The man who killed my contact is still afoot and determined to have his revenge for my role in keeping Napoleon on Elba. I have been foolish by letting my feelings for you be known. I fear that he will try to get to me through you."

Isabella's expression soften. "I'm sorry. I should not have said what I did. You've never shirked your duty, whatever you saw that duty as being." She sighed and reached for his hand, tracing the scar with her finger tip. The anger between them faded. "You told me the truth. I should have reacted better. No wonder you didn't want to tell me." She looked up into his face. "How did we get to this, Tristan? You went away to save me and I married another to save you."

Tristan stepped close. "I should have asked you to run away and you should have kissed me. We've been at cross purposes, my love." He drew her into the circle of his arms and embraced her. The balance between them was restored and perhaps even more than restored. "Does this mean you'll consider my proposal? I can't erase the rumors Beatrix started. They are true although exceedingly exaggerated. I can't tell anyone my true purpose. No one can know, Isabella. After this assignment, I'll simply be Viscount Gresham. I've told you the truth." When Isabella nodded her consent, he tipped her chin up and continued in a more playful vein.

"I've told you my secret. Now, you tell me yours or else I'll have a bit of blackmail to urge you to the altar with."

Isabella looked at him quizzically. "Whatever are you talking about?"

Tristan reached into a pocket. "I'm talking about a black glove a secret admirer left." He dangled the glove in front of her.

"Left? You stole it." Isabella flushed with embarrassment. "When did you know it was me? I thought I'd disguised myself quite well."

Tristan smiled. "It wasn't until the second meeting. You couldn't quite cover up your scent of roses and you used a gesture that you'd used with me down at the duck pond."

"I wanted answers and since none were forthcoming from you, I decided to try and get them another way," Isabella confessed. "It was your undoing though. I could hardly countenance the rakish man who met with me. He was so different than the friend who humbly begged me to help him find a wife."

"I only took Alain's suggestion that you help me find a wife so that I had an excuse to be in your company. It's you I've wanted all along, Bella." Tristan bent down to retrieve his coat and give it a quick brush with his hand. "Come along, it's getting too dark to be out here and dinner should be ready by now."

Hands linked, they strolled back to the manor, silently enjoying the quiet evening descending around them.

Tristan's prediction was correct. They had two weeks of idyllic peace. They had their routine. They rode in the mornings and spent time in the stables acquainting themselves with the few horses still there. In the afternoons, Isabella went over household accounts and talked with the housekeeper about preparations for the house party. Tristan looked over estate business and rode out to see his tenants. In the evenings they played cards or reminisced over old times at Summer Hill.

For Isabella, this was a glorious time suspended from reality. Tristan loved her; she had her answers to the myriad of riddles surrounding him. She would have to come to grips with the scandal. Tristan could not dispute the rumors without exposing himself as an agent and even then, the kernels of truth embedded in the rumors would only make arguing them worse. The important thing was that she was now free to love him. He had trusted her with the truth. She would trust him with her heart. She was beginning to realize she'd wagered more than a horse on Valentine's day. She'd bet her very soul.

As the days wore on, Tristan began to believe he could persuade her, that Isabella could come to terms with his past and his motivations. The Isabella who dressed in his mother's old gowns and rode recklessly with her hair down loved him. He was sure of it. At some point, who he'd been and who he'd become had ceased to be important to her. All that mattered was who he was now. Tristan's heart soared. Joy was within his grasp. There were still some things to tell her, but they could wait until the intrigue of the house party was put to rest and they could get on with their life together.

The day of the house party dawned bright and clear for the end of March. Last minute preparations for the guests who would arrive late in the afternoon kept Isabella running pillar to post until the first carriage wheels were heard crunching on the gravel drive. She preferred it that way, otherwise she'd think too much about the impending events. If all went well and the informant was caught, she could look forward to having her betrothal to Tristan announced at the hunt ball. She dared not think about the consequences of not catching the informant and what that would imply. Just as she dared not ponder the news Alain had brought when he arrived earlier. Avery Driscoll had asked permission to seek her hand in marriage.

As luck would have it, Beatrix Smallwood was among the first to arrive. "Gresham! I am so glad to see you." Her unmistakable voice rang out as she exited gracefully from her traveling coach.

Isabella noted the guarded expression that came over Tristan's face. She had not been invited and clearly Tristan had not expected her attendance. She'd ridden down with the earl of Middleton, whom Isabella had invited in hopes that he'd bring Hellion along with him.

Tristan performed his duties as best he could. "Lady Westbrooke, you recall Mrs. Smallwood. Mrs. Smallwood, Lady Westbrooke is acting as hostess for me."

"Gresham darling, I'd have been your hostess if you'd but asked," Beatrix Smallwood gushed, boldly linking her arm through Tristan's.

Isabella was furious. How dare Tristan bring his former mistress out here to flaunt! She wanted to scratch the woman's eyes out. Then a cold smile flitted across her lips. "Mrs. Smallwood, how good to see you again. I hope you ride? It will be nice to have another woman on the hunt. So few women truly ride these days."

Beatrix matched Isabella's smile. "I can hold my own," Beatrix replied to the veiled challenge, patting Tristan's arm possessively.

"Are you certain?" Isabella responded coolly, unfazed by Beatrix's innuendo.

"Quite certain, Lady Westbrooke," Beatrix said coyly,

looking up at Tristan from under her dark lashes. "I am told I have an excellent seat."

Isabella ignored the woman's outrageous comment and strode over to see Hellion.

Isabella surveyed the gathering as they played charades and cards in the drawing room after supper. The party was off to a good start. The guests were mingling amiably, even those guests whose arrivals had taken her by surprise; there had been two.

Obviously, neither she nor Tristan had anticipated Beatrix's arrival. But Mrs. Smallwood was on her best behavior so far, as were the other guests.

The only fly in the ointment so far was that Beatrix had managed to dominate Tristan's attention all evening with sly glances and meaningful touches as she passed him. Isabella had wanted Tristan to put Beatrix in her place, to tell her that he had proposed to Isabella. But it was unfair to expect Tristan to put himself out so far when he had other concerns on his mind. And of course it wouldn't do to have such news get out without first talking with Avery.

At the moment, Avery was entertaining the lovely young Caroline Danvers while her ambitious mother looked on with beaming approval. Lady Danvers was an old friend of her mother's who lived close by. Isabella walked over to speak with him. Avery smiled at her and Isabella knew he was thinking she'd crossed the room to speak with him. Perhaps walking over to the group had been a mistake. She didn't want to suddenly be left alone with Avery. Caroline saved her.

"Lady Westbrooke, thank you so much for inviting me!" Caroline was genuinely grateful. She was young and had only been out one year, but she was pretty with blond ringlets and blue eyes.

"It is my pleasure to have you, Caroline. Have you met Viscount Gresham yet?" Isabella inquired, aware of the predatory gleam igniting in Lady Danvers's eye at the mention of their host.

"Not yet. We arrived late and he was already engaged with the gentlemen."

"Come with me, I will introduce you now," Isabella offered, knowing it would keep her from being alone with Avery and a potentially awkward conversation.

When the clock struck eleven, Isabella rose to signal that it would be appropriate to retire for the evening. She saw to the guests and their comforts before taking her own candle and heading upstairs for bed. The exhausting day had been a success. At the foot of the stairs, Tristan waited for her, chatting glibly with Giles and Alain.

"Here's my hostess now," he said when she neared. "You've done a splendid job, Bella. I feel like a guest at my own party. There's nothing for me to do."

"You were the perfect host," Isabella returned. "Thank you for taking time with Caroline. She wanted to meet you so very much."

"She's a nice girl. I enjoyed talking with her. I have wanted to meet her ever since I traded names with Alain at the Valentine's party." Tristan crooked his arm. "Let's go up. Tomorrow will be busy with the hunt and the ball. If I know you, Isabella, you'll be up early and in the stables before anyone else."

The morning dawned gray but dry. The overcast weather would be perfect for hunting, Isabella noted, pulling back the curtains at her window. She dressed quickly in a dark green riding habit with breeches underneath and headed for the stables. Last night, Middleton had consented to let her ride the stallion. She was in alt.

Isabella stopped inside the stable door and inhaled the fragrance of horseflesh. Hay and horse were comforting smells to her. She proceeded to Hellion's stall and fished a slice of apple from her pocket. She held it on her flat palm and offered it to the horse. He whickered and then ate. She petted him and spoke to him in reassuring tones before leading him out to curry and saddle. She hummed as she worked, so absorbed in her task that she didn't notice anyone enter the stables until a pair of boots caught her eye while she picked Hellion's hooves. Hellion's nostril's flared.

"Alain is right, Isabella, that horse is half-wild," Tristan said in greeting.

"Good morning." Isabella looked up from grooming Hellion. She critically surveyed Tristan. Did the man have to look so good all the time? He cut a superb figure, as he well knew, in his riding attire and polished boots, swinging a crop at his side.

"I assume you're riding him today. I think it's folly to try and handle such an animal from a side saddle," Tristan advised.

"I agree. I am not using a side saddle." Isabella smiled and lifted her skirts to her knees. "I'll be riding astride. I have it on good authority that you appreciate a rider with a fine seat. I wanted to make sure mine was amply on display."

"About Beatrix, I didn't know she was going to be here," Tristan began. "I hope this doesn't alter our plans to announce the betrothal tonight?"

"You must catch the informant, Tristan. That is our foremost concern. I must know that you're safe," Isabella reminded him, worry evident in her eyes.

"I agree, but I am not sure that he's here. He should have a scar, just a faint one on his cheek where I nicked him. I know everyone here and none of them bear the mark. I don't want to waste our ball because he didn't show up." Tristan grinned wickedly and stepped closer. Isabella knew he would have kissed her if other hunters hadn't appeared in the stable at that moment to claim their mounts. Reluctantly, she drew back and made a great show of grooming Hellion.

Within a few moments, the stable was the scene of orderly chaos as grooms hurried to saddle horses. When all was ready, Isabella mounted Hellion next to Tristan in the yard as everyone assembled to drink from the hunt cup and to hear the master of the hunt blow his horn. Then they were off with Hellion leading the way. She was in high spirits. Tristan was safe for the moment. The informant hadn't shown up. Beatrix made a bid early in the hunt to ride in the front of the pack with Isabella and the other neck-or-nothing riders but soon found Hellion out of her league and dropped back to ride with Middleton, much to Isabella's gratification.

By the time the hunt ball commenced that evening, Isabella felt her world had finally started to right itself. There was little chance of danger tonight. She could revel in the moment. She looked down the staircase before she descended. Tristan stood in the hall chatting with Caroline Danvers. He was wearing the celery waistcoat with silver buttons that Isabella had gamely sent him, under a black evening coat with black trousers.

He turned and smiled up at her. His eyes raked her appreciatively. Isabella knew she'd chosen her gown of dark green velvet wisely. Tristan beckoned for her to join him and she sailed down the stairs to his side. She didn't leave his side until eleven o'clock when he quietly whispered he had to go. She looked at him strangely. He had not said where he was going or what he was doing, but she nodded her consent, her eyes following him until he was out of sight. When he did not return in fifteen minutes, she went looking for him.

Chapter Twelve

Isabella glanced around in the hall for some clue as to where Tristan had gone. A crack of light coming from underneath the estate office drew her attention. As she neared, muted voices reached her ears. Tristan was not alone. She pushed open the door and halted at the sight of Beatrix, Middleton and Tristan. Middleton sat behind the massive desk. Beatrix perched on the arm of Tristan's chair at an awkward angle. Tristan's back was to her. Beatrix turned and Isabella gasped. Beatrix held a naked blade in her hand. She must have had it held against Tristan's neck. It would explain her awkward angle. She realized Tristan's hands were tied.

"Come in, we've been expecting you." Beatrix waved the blade, gesturing to the empty chair next to Tristan.

"What is going on in here?" Isabella demanded with all the authority she could muster while her mind grappled with the situation.

"Sit down." Beatrix returned the blade to Tristan's neck and pressed. A small bead of blood shone red. "I mean business tonight, my lady."

Isabella sat. Her worry for Tristan overrode any fear she might have for herself. "Are you hurt?" she asked Tristan.

Beatrix exploded. "This is not a garden party, Lady

Westbrooke. I am the hostess here. You will not speak unless I instruct you to do so. Failure to follow my instructions will cause things to go poorly for your man, although I doubt you'll be so willing to claim him when we're finished tonight."

"You will not kill us," Isabella challenged haughtily. If she'd learned anything in her years as the marchioness it was to not show fear. She'd been a young hostess who'd had to prove herself. She'd stared down more than one supercilious matron in her day. This coarse, coldhearted woman who dressed herself in finery and masqueraded as acceptable Society would not cow her.

"There's more than one way to kill, my lady." Middleton rose from the chair behind the desk and came around to lean on the corner of the massive structure. "Knives and pistols are sometimes too easy."

Isabella would give a monkey to know what Middleton was doing in the center of all this drama. He was a single-minded sportsman who spent his time in the country to hunt and ride. When he wasn't in the country, he was traveling to exotic locales for the hunting there. *Supposedly*. With a flash of insight, she thought he might as well have been in France. No one truly knew if he'd actually gone on to Germany or wherever else he purported to go.

Beatrix chimed in. "Yes, there's more than one way to kill. One doesn't have to die to be dead. One can go through the motions of living and still be dead inside. That is indeed a great torture, to know you have year after endless year to live with your empty self. Isn't that right, Tristan? It's what you did to me, and now I'll return the favor."

She kicked him hard in the leg for good measure. Tristan winced. That was when Isabella noticed his legs were tied as well. However did they manage to get Tristan trussed up like a goose?

Beatrix read her thoughts. "We knocked him out, my dear Lady Westbrooke. Middleton lured him away from the ballroom and I coshed him on the head from behind. We'd have never subdued him otherwise. You do know he's famous for his fighting abilities in our dark circles?" Beatrix stood up and began to walk the carpet that lay in front of the desk, content that she had Isabella's compliance for the moment.

"You see, Lady Westbrooke, the good viscount is a private agent for the Crown. He performs all kinds of nasty deeds under the cover of being a social buffoon, who is only good at wooing ladies and giving fabulous parties."

Isabella felt triumphant. "I know that. Tristan has discussed his military career with me." She was aware of their game now. They wanted to turn her from Tristan. When Tristan had said he worried about the informant using her as leverage, she had thought only of a kidnapping. But now she knew what Beatrix and Middleton meant when they'd said there was more than one way to kill. If this was to be a game of wits, Isabella was well armed.

Beatrix gave a cold smile. "Ah, so you know. Do you know everything? Do you know that he killed my brother?"

Isabella cast a brief look at Tristan. He too was surprised by the news. It was the first time he'd spoken since she'd entered the room. "Don't tell lies, Beatrix. I don't even know your brother or that you have one."

Beatrix's eyes narrowed dangerously. "The man on the docks in Paris was my brother. Tall, golden haired and young. You sent him home bleeding. He died three days later."

"He ambushed me with two others. He knew the risks. Treason is not a game played for cheap stakes."

"Nonetheless, I loved him," Beatrix spat back. She turned her cold blue eyes on Isabella. "You love your brother as well. We have something in common. Perhaps I will have done you a favor by the end of the evening. Moreland killed my brother, and he came here to hunt yours. When Tristan was busy confessing his many sins to you did he mention that one of his leading suspects was your brother, Baron Wickham?"

"Alain? Whatever for?" Isabella cried in shock. She looked to Tristan for a plausible explanation, but it was Beatrix who spoke.

"All he had to go on was a physical description of the intruder who'd broken into the town house and whatever physical characteristics he could recall from the melee at the docks. I believe your brother matches the description ideally."

"So do numerous other men!" Isabella retorted. She followed Beatrix's gaze as it moved to Middleton.

"Exactly," Beatrix purred in satisfaction. "As you've guessed, Middleton and Wickham are of the same height and general features as my brother. But Alain made the mistake of visiting Moreland's town house and actually showing interest in the cards. He even took some one evening when Moreland was away. Your brother made it easy to frame him by spending so much time away at undisclosed locations. It would have been lovely to actually see Tristan send his dear friend and his betrothed's brother to his demise, but we needed the cards for ourselves. So we'll have to settle for having swiped the information and upsetting Tristan's marriage plans."

Isabella's stomach churned at the story Beatrix spun. Surely, Tristan hadn't really thought the informant was Alain? Beatrix was cruel. It was not beyond her to fabricate a story to fit her needs. Isabella stiffened her spine. She would not give Beatrix the satisfaction of seeing her discomfort. "Why are you doing this? I think you risk much for very little in return."

"There is nothing little about revenge!" Beatrix shot back. "He murdered my brother and he foiled plans to put the rightful emperor of France back in power."

Isabella turned to the silent Middleton. "What of you, sir? What do you stand to gain by abetting such treason?"

Middleton said nothing but Isabella could guess. He was besotted with Beatrix. He had hardly taken his eyes from her. He probably promised to marry her and make her his countess. Isabella couldn't imagine why Beatrix would consent to marry a man whose pockets were to let. Then she recalled the information in the coded cards. They weren't collecting it for their own use, they were collecting it to sell to someone else.

"I am rich," Isabella said, mostly for Middleton's benefit. "Sell me the information for three times the price your connection was paying you."

"Why would you want it?" Middleton asked curiously, his interest piqued by that sum of money.

"I don't want it. It means nothing to me," Isabella said with a casual air. "But you need money, both of you do. If you sell the information to me, I'll destroy the cards and there will be no threat of being caught and tried for treason. There will be no proof." She could see Middleton weighing the possibilities. She could practically read his mind. He could afford to marry Beatrix and he could stay in England. No doubt they would have to start up somewhere else after this latest deal.

"No. That is not the plan," Beatrix said sharply to Middleton. "That information is needed to help free Napoleon. We need the shipping schedules."

Tristan joined the verbal fray. "What if the information is false? Then you will be hunted by those you are trying to help and you'll have turned down a great sum of money."

Middleton bolted upright from his lazy pose at the desk. "What are you saying? Have you been feeding false information?"

"Perhaps, but then again it might all be true. Beatrix stole information from me before. She knows the information in the 'love notes' was true once."

Beatrix pressed the knife hard against Tristan's skin,

breaking it. Blood welled. Isabella stifled a scream. If she screamed Tristan would be dead before help could reach them. "Tell them the truth, Tristan," she urged.

"Wait." A malicious grin spread across Middleton's face as he stepped forward. "You're going around it all wrong, Bea. When hunting, one learns that animals only give themselves up to save their young or their mates. Gresham here will never tell you the truth if it's only his neck at risk. But the lovely Lady Westbrooke's is another story."

Beatrix's hand relaxed on the knife hilt. She gave Middleton a flirtatious look. "That assumes he cares a whit for her." She turned her gaze on Isabella. "Do you think Tristan will rescue you? Does he love you enough to pick you over his duty to his country? It may be that he only pretended to care about you in order to get close to you. Maybe he thought you'd let something slip about Alain that would confirm his suspicions." She left Tristan's side and moved to Isabella, where she bent to Isabella's ear. "If I had to pick between his neck and mine, I'd pick mine. Tristan's a lost cause, my lady."

"Ah, my Beatrix, you weave a web like no other!" Middleton applauded. "But we must go before anyone begins to miss the pair of them. They have a betrothal to announce tonight, if I am not mistaken. That is, if the lady will still have the scoundrel." Middleton made a clucking noise through his teeth. "It is a shame to wed someone you can't truly trust, my lady.

"What shall it be, Beatrix, shall we take the money and turn the information over or shall we gamble on it?" Middleton inquired.

"We shall gamble on it. My only regret is that we are not slitting Moreland's throat."

"Bea, he's slit his own throat and saved us the trouble," Middleton laughed as he raised the window sash and helped Beatrix climb through. "Now you, Lady Westbrooke. We need some insurance that Tristan won't come after us. You'll not be harmed, merely inconvenienced, unless Tristan decides to play unfairly." Middleton waved a pistol casually as he gestured towards the window. "Give us two hours, Moreland. After that, we'll leave the lady at an inn with coach fare to a destination of her choice. But it will go poorly for her if you decide to play the hero, assuming you get out of that chair any time soon."

Isabella had no choice but to go with them. She climbed through the window and shot Tristan a parting glance. She'd hoped to see some sign of emotion in his face, but his demeanor was stoic and unreadable.

Three horses were waiting outside. Middleton gave her a leg up on Hellion and a warning. "Don't think to use his speed to escape. I have no love for this horse and his temper. I'll shoot him out from under you, make no mistake about it."

Beatrix cooed evilly in the darkness. "She wouldn't want to miss the fun, George. We've handed her the ultimate litmus test. If Tristan breaks the rules and comes after her, she'll know he loved her more than his work. If he doesn't come, she'll know where his true motivations lay."

The trio rode in silence, all of them with their ears trained on the sounds of the night. They listened for the thunder of following hooves. None came. Isabella did her best to keep her thoughts away from the cutting remarks Beatrix had made. Mrs. Smallwood was wrong. The Tristan Isabella knew was a deeply honorable man. He had not used her to get to Alain. She strained her ears for any sound of his horse behind them. She told herself that there were many reasons why Tristan would not follow, especially since her safety was at stake.

An hour into the ride, reality set in. She could not trust Beatrix and Middleton to keep their word about her safe return. Beatrix was a conniving woman who covered her tracks. Why would she allow Isabella to go free when Isabella could show others the course they'd taken and make a good guess as to where they would go? If she could figure that out, Tristan could, too. That meant he would come. But he did not.

In the end, Isabella saw an opening to save herself. Beatrix and Middleton stopped at a *Y* in the road and began arguing about the route. Isabella kicked Hellion hard and took off cross country in the direction from which they'd come. She no longer had any fear of Middleton's pistol. They meant to do away with her anyway. She would rather be shot trying to escape than to simply wait for the inevitable.

Hellion surged beneath her. Despite the danger she faced, Isabella reveled in the strength of the stallion beneath her. He could run for hours. She had sensed it earlier that day during the hunt. She hazarded a glance behind and saw Middleton in pursuit. Middleton rode a fresh horse that hadn't hunted that morning. The bay was a prime goer, but with Middleton's weight, the gelding couldn't race forever. Isabella urged Hellion on to greater lengths. She didn't worry about Middleton ever catching up and pulling alongside, but she did worry about Middleton getting close enough to fire a shot.

Isabella's route paralleled the road. Now, as Hellion pounded forwarded, a stone fence and stile loomed in the near distance. There was no question of stopping to go through the stile or riding along the fence until an opening appeared. The only course of action was to go over it. This was the chance Isabella had been waiting for. She had jumped Hellion twice during the hunt, although the jumps hadn't been as high. But she knew the strength of his legs. He could take the fence. She was certain the gelding would not be able to clear it. She gave Hellion the signal with her knees, felt his powerful haunches bunch and they were airborne.

With a whoop of glee, Isabella and Hellion landed solidly on the other side and kept running. A last glance behind assured her that the wall had stopped Middleton on his gelding. She slowed Hellion to a canter. A mile later she met the rescue party which had set out from The Meadows. Alain was among them, riding neck-or-nothing in the dark and risking his prized hunter. All she could think about when she slid off Hellion into Alain's brotherly embrace was that Tristan had not come.

She was furious and devastated. Her mind gave free rein to the doubts Beatrix had so skillfully provoked earlier. She could not go back to The Meadows. She begged Alain to take her to a nearby inn.

As she had expected, sleep would not come as her mind replayed the whole ghastly evening from the moment Tristan had smiled up at her from the staircase. Hours later as the pink fingers of sunrise stroked the dark sky, she trembled violently, not from the danger of her gallant ride but from the overwhelming betrayal she'd suffered at Tristan's hands. She had been petrified to see him tied to the chair with a knife pressed to his neck. He had apparently not shared her fear.

She sat by the window of her room for hours, dazed and still dressed in her muddied ball gown until Alain came to report the denouement of the evening's spectacle to her. She listened dispassionately to his news.

Beatrix and Middleton had escaped them under cover of darkness, the search party having lost ground when they had stopped upon finding her safe. The riders who continued on ahead could not catch Middleton and Beatrix who had spied them in time to keep a considerable distance between them. Worse, it appeared that they had split ways. They were both at large.

Alain volunteered no news of Tristan and Isabella was too dejected to ask. She rallied her last resources of strength. She washed, called for a private post chaise and before going back to London, returned Hellion to The Meadows with Alain. She took nothing with her but her small valise and her misery. She would go back to London for the Season, stay long enough to not look as if she were running away and then retire to the country, perhaps for good. Inside, she felt dead.

*   *   *

Tristan pushed his horse the last three miles to London, relief coursing through him as the outskirts of town came into view just as dusk fell. He'd ridden hard the moment the last of his guests had quit The Meadows. His departure hadn't been soon enough to suit his tastes. He had not slept since the night before the hunt. Exhaustion threatened to claim him but he wouldn't concede to the physical limits of his body until he saw Isabella.

Alain had told him Bella had taken a post chaise back to London when he'd returned at noon with Hellion. Since then, Tristan had hurried his remaining guests out the door and saddled the freshest horse left in his stable.

Tristan turned the horse towards Westbrooke House. He would have to report to Whitehall also before going home to sleep. That could wait. Isabella could not. Many things needed explaining. Not the least being why he hadn't ridden out after her with the rescue party. The knock on the head he'd suffered had rendered him too dizzy to ride and the tightness of the bonds about his legs had effectively numbed them. When he'd risen to join the search party, he'd collapsed into near unconsciousness. Only Alain's firm grip had kept him upright. Isabella had to know that and the myriad of other things he'd waited too long to tell her.

Tristan slid off his mount's back and bounded up the steps to Westbrooke House, impatiently seizing the knocker. Regis answered. "I am here to see Lady Westbrooke," Tristan said, nearly breathless from his efforts.

Regis nodded, dour faced and closed the door. Endless minutes later, he returned. "I am sorry, Lady Westbrooke is not at home."

"Where did she go? When will she be back? I must speak with her. I know she will see me," Tristan protested.

Regis gave him a pointed look. "I am sorry, my lord. She is not at home to you."

The door shut and Tristan stared at it in shock. Isabella

would not receive him. The enormity of her rejection flooded him, overwhelmed him so that he stumbled down the steps to his horse. Short of yelling up at her from the streets, there was nothing more he could do that day. Surely after she had some time to put events into perspective, she would agree to see him. The thought brought him a bit of hope. He would go to Whitehall, then to sleep. Everything would look better in the morning.

The offices at Whitehall were mostly deserted, the clerks and aides having gone home hours ago to warm suppers. But a light still glowed from under the door of the man Tristan wanted to see. He had suspected as much. Halsey worked alone and late. He rapped on the door and called out, "It's Moreland."

"I've been expecting you," Halsey said after Tristan had taken a seat in a battered leather chair.

The small office in the bowels of Whitehall was crowded with stacks of papers and files. Tristan marveled that Halsey could find anything there. Then again, it wouldn't be unlikely that a spy would not be able to find anything either.

"The mission is complete," Tristan said in terse tones, holding Halsey's gaze.

"I heard it ended messily. Are you all right?"

"I am well enough. I have a goose egg on the back of my head and my left hand is temporarily useless, but I am whole otherwise." Tristan leaned back in the chair and crossed his legs. He wasn't surprised Halsey had heard rumors of the house party already. Some of his houseguests had left at daybreak, eager to be the first back to Town with the latest gossip and Halsey had ears everywhere. What he didn't have were the facts. That was why Tristan came.

"The double agent was really a duo, Beatrix and her brother. Her brother was the third assailant I faced on the Paris wharf. The wound I inflicted on him was indeed fatal, although we had no way of verifying that. Beatrix knew though. She knew her brother was dead and she knew we were unsure of who he was or whether or not he lived. Hence, her need for Middleton." Tristan laid out the convoluted plan.

"Ah, another man ensnared by Beatrix's wiles," Halsey mused.

"Middleton isn't quite as innocent as that," Tristan corrected. "He has dabbled in petty espionage to line his purse before. But Beatrix and her offer are by far the largest opportunities he's had. Beatrix asked him to pose as the double agent since she knew we had a vague description of the man: tall, blond, athletic in build. She also convinced him to steal the cards from my town house."

"I see how it falls into place now." Halsey steepled his hands. "Beatrix almost succeeded on both levels. She almost got away with her plan to steal information and she almost succeeded in exacting her vengeance against you."

Tristan nodded. "I was very close to believing the culprit was Alain Hartsfield, my dear friend. I was convinced the Home Office wanted me on the assignment because they already suspected Alain and wanted to use me to get close to him. Beatrix had set up so many different layers to her plan, it is mind boggling. I regret that she escaped, but we have the knowledge we set out to find. We know who the double agent is and that renders her powerless."

A slow smile spread across Halsey's face. "You're partly wrong. We have the information and we have Beatrix. She was apprehended in Southhampton just a few hours ago. Luckily for us, there were no boats sailing until the evening tide. Once I heard the rumors trickling back into the city about your house party, I sent my fastest riders out."

"That is the best news I've heard today," Tristan said honestly. Knowing that Beatrix had been apprehended relieved his worry that Isabella would still be threatened. "What about Middleton?"

"He is still at large, but as you said, he's a petty player in intrigue. I expect we won't hear from him again. He'll be too worried about his own safety to surface any time soon."

Tristan had to agree. From all accounts, Middleton had been Beatrix's stooge. He rose. "Then I give you good night. I have ridden hard and slept little. I will see to it that you have a full written report shortly, followed by my official resignation as planned."

Tristan departed Whitehall feeling lighter of step. True, there were still several items to work out with Isabella, but knowing the assignment was over helped lighten his burden considerably. Tomorrow, he would try again.

He did not succeed the next day nor the day after that or the day after that. Each day he went to Isabella's home and found himself denied access. He plagued her with messages and errand boys bearing bouquets of flowers and boxes of bonbons. His frustration grew. After a week, he tried a new tack and attended any ball or event she might possibly be at even though it meant attending three events a night on some evenings.

He allied himself with people connected to Isabella, in hopes of catching news of her. He spent evenings with groups including Lady Briarton, the overly perfect Avery Driscoll and Isabella's protégé, Caroline Danvers. But none of the associations brought him closer to Isabella. She was absent from their ranks, although Caroline valiantly tried to fill the void so that he didn't feel the odd man out.

Indeed, Tristan appreciated her efforts. It was somewhat unnerving to move in Isabella's circles without her. He had not realized how much she had paved his way back into Society upon his return. Now, with the news about the house party and his true role in the event being revealed, he was something of a hero. Mothers beat a path to him with their daughters in tow and Tristan was happy to let Caroline act as a buffer.

He danced with her often at the events since it precluded having to dance with debutantes he didn't know and didn't want to know. Caroline was a companionable ally, ready to make conversation as they danced and just as ready to give him silence if he needed it. When they did talk, they talked of horses and the countryside.

Tristan saw nothing untoward in their association. Perhaps that was why the rumors startled him so much. Matrons began to comment on the time he and Caroline spent in one another's company, how regularly he danced with her, the mere daughter of a simple country gentleman. It came as a surprise to him that speculation was growing among both genders in regards to him and Caroline. Most people expected he would offer for her.

At first he ignored the rumors. But Isabella's continued absence and rejection weighed heavily on him. She had washed her hands of him and it was time to realize he was facing life without her a second time. His hope in tatters, Tristan was desperate to assuage the hurt left by Isabella's desertion. If he remained alone and unattached, he would always yearn for her. The torture would be exquisite if she became the wife of another and he was left alone. The torture would be unbearable if she chose to remain unmarried, choosing a single life over a life with him. Either way, Tristan knew he would burn in the deepest levels of hell if either of those scenarios came to pass.

In the darkest watches of the night, he convinced himself the only way to repair his heart would be to put himself beyond Isabella's reach forever and marry another; someone who expected only companionship from him; someone who might not guess his motives for marriage. Armed with resolve, Tristan watched the sun rise on another sleepless night.

When the shops opened, he went to a jeweler of good repute and purchased a ring sure to impress even the most reluctant fathers and went to pay his call. The moment the ring was in his hand, he felt a certain numbness start to claim him. Isabella was slipping away and with her, the fire of his being. She had been his purpose for so long, he was at a loss.

He reminded himself numbness was good. It dulled the pain and eventually, it would overcome the ache. He turned down Brook Street and climbed the steps to the Danvers' residence. Caroline was as good a choice as any and better than most.

Chapter Thirteen

London, mid-May

It had been six weeks since Tristan's house party and Isabella could put Avery Driscoll off no longer. He had patiently waited the two weeks she'd originally requested for an answer regarding his proposal. Then he had politely waited without pressing her, believing that her ordeal at Gresham's house party had overset her more than she let on.

Tonight, he would wait no longer. Avery had very specifically asked her to attend his Aunt Elizabeth's ball that evening in hopes of resolving their relationship. Isabella knew she owed him that courtesy in return for the numerous courtesies he had shown her throughout the tenure of their friendship.

She looked at her pale face in the mirror as she sat listlessly holding her hairbrush at her vanity. Tristan had left her ravaged. She promised herself that she would not leave Avery in the same condition. She did not want this miserable half life for him. She knew Avery hoped that she would accept him and that the ball could become an occasion for announcing their betrothal. In all fairness, she could not accept his honest proposal. She could not burden him with her broken heart. Avery would spend his life devoting himself to the impossible task of making her happy, of making her forget Tristan Moreland. She would not see him become the victim of unrequited love.

Since the house party, she had neither been out to any of the usual routs or musicales nor had she received any callers since her return to town. She had shopped a few times with Amy to keep up some semblance of appearances and ridden in the park with Alain. Beyond that, she relied on Regis and Betty for information. Tristan had called several times the first two weeks of her reclusivity. But she could not bring herself to see him. She would most likely have to face him tonight and that would be hard enough. She hoped seeing him in public would give her the strength she needed to get through the evening. If she could get through the evening, she could get through the next evening and the next when they would all inevitably be together.

And they would be together unless she chose to shun all society forever. According to Alain's news, Tristan was doing well. He was a hero these days since his part in the mission to catch Beatrix and Middleton became public. Everyone forgave his supposed behavior with Beatrix, understanding that it had all been a role played for the greater good.

Amy brought similar tidings as well. Tristan was a hero and the reticence any doting fathers might have had about letting Tristan court their daughters had vanished. He was the most eligible bachelor on the dance floors these days. Unlike Isabella, who sequestered herself away, Tristan was at every function, even two or three a night. He danced with everyone, but particularly with Caroline Danvers. Amy's eyes had sparkled at the mention, saying, "Isabella, you might win that wager yet. There's still three weeks until June. Speculation is rife that he will offer for the lovely Caroline."

She had listened to the news dispassionately, telling herself she cared not a whit who Tristan danced with or who he might propose to. She was doubly glad that she had not shared

Tristan's proposal with anyone. She would have looked foolish now that his affections were engaged elsewhere.

Isabella stood and rang for Betty. It was time to dress and Avery deserved to have her looking her best. She selected one of her favorite gowns of sage-colored velvet trimmed in a deep forest green that she'd worn only one other time.

She arrived at the ball alone, but Avery had been on the watch for her and promptly left his aunt's side in the receiving line when he spotted her in the queue. He was impeccably dressed as usual and he graciously stayed at her side until they reached his aunt, keeping up an excellent stream of small talk that succeeded in putting her at ease. Whatever his hopes were for the evening, Avery was clearly dedicated to her happiness first and foremost.

"Please, don't let me keep you from your hosting duties," Isabella offered after Avery introduced her to his Aunt Elizabeth, Lady Sizemore.

"You are my hosting duty, Isabella," Avery whispered confidentially, covering her gloved hand with his. "My cousin is filling in for me admirably." He nodded to where a dark-haired gentleman had taken up residence next to Lady Sizemore. "The dancing will begin in a few minutes. I'd hoped to claim the first dance?"

Isabella smiled for Avery's benefit. "Of course, I'd be honored. I'll make a quick trip to the retiring room and be back before the dancing starts." Isabella ascended the staircase in search of the ladies retiring rooms. She didn't need to check her dress or shoes but a trip upstairs would help her gather her thoughts and put on her social face. As she entered the chamber, Caroline Danvers waved enthusiastically to her.

"Lady Westbrooke, I am so glad you're here! I have the most wonderful piece of news to share with you." Caroline left the small group of girls and crossed the room to her side. Isabella pasted on a smile she didn't feel and gave Caroline all her attention.

"It is still a secret, but not for much longer. I have to tell you since you have been my mentor." Caroline rushed over her words in obvious excitement, her voice low and private.

"Whatever is your news, Caroline?" Isabella encouraged as her head spun trying to keep up with the excited girl. Caroline glowed tonight, looking young and sophisticated in the stylish pale blue gown Isabella had recommended for her.

"It's the Viscount Gresham." She paused and blushed. "Tristan." She said his name tentatively, as if still trying the word out on her tongue. "He proposed to me today and I have accepted. Mama and Papa are thrilled and we have you to thank," Caroline gushed, squeezing Isabella's hands until they hurt. "He says he wants a wedding before June is over. He doesn't want to wait. Isn't that romantic?"

Isabella looked at Caroline's expectant blue eyes, filled with joy over her upcoming nuptials. She managed to mumble appropriate niceties and disengage herself from Caroline before desperation completely claimed her. In a daze, she found some privacy and sat down heavily. Tristan to marry Caroline! She had been warned, several times in fact. Alain had told her. Amy had told her of Tristan dancing regular attendance on Caroline. She had heard and done nothing to fix his attentions back on her. She should be glad. Caroline loved horses and the country life. They would be well suited.

Faint strains of the orchestra tuning up downstairs, reminding her of her promise to meet Avery. She gathered her skirts and pinched her cheeks, trying to hide her bleeding heart with a smile.

She saw Alain on the steps as she descended. He waved up at her and came to her side immediately, kissing her cheek. "Are you well, Bella? I am glad to see you out at last," he said quietly.

"I am fine, Alain. And you?"

"Tristan made all the arrangements to exonerate me and keep it hushed up. There's nothing to fear." He reassured her with a pat on the hand. "He's here tonight, you know. He said he called at the house to see you when he returned to Town but you refused to see him." The expression on his face suggested he hoped for further clarification or confession from his sister regarding her situation with Tristan. He was to be dissatisfied.

"I saw Caroline Danvers earlier," Isabella said, redirecting the conversation.

"Then you've heard the news?"

Isabella nodded, a weary look on her face mingled with the hurt she was clearly trying to hide.

"I am sorry." Alain's own expression mirrored his sister's hurt. "I don't pretend to understand all there was between you and Tristan. But I feel something akin to what you're feeling. Tristan is a changed man. He has been a true friend in every way possible regarding the clearance of my name. Yet, I know that our friendship is altered and there is dissonance between us, over you."

"I never wanted to come between you and Tristan. I know how much his friendship means to you, has always meant to you," Isabella whispered in consolation.

Alain began to speak but at that moment Avery spotted her on the stairs and came up to join them, cutting off any further conversation. "Wickham! So glad you could come." He greeted Alain effusively. By the look of happiness on his face, Isabella knew he obviously took her brother's presence as a sign of her acceptance. The orchestra started and he turned to Isabella. "Shall we?"

She was happy to accept in order to steer Avery away from Alain. She had not discussed her situation with Alain and did not want him taken by surprise or caught off guard by Avery's assumptions. The opening dance was a country reel and Isabella threw herself into the steps in the hopes of distracting her thoughts from Tristan. Afterwards, Avery suggested a stroll on the verandah. Once they were alone, he turned towards her, ready to broach the issue that had been at the forefront of his mind.

"I have meant to give you time to consider my proposal. If your answer is favorable, I'd like to have our engagement announced tonight. It would thrill my aunt to no end," Avery began. "However, I do not want you to feel pushed. I am sure the ordeal at Gresham's haunts you still."

Tristan was beyond her reach now, but some modicum of happiness was still within her reach, Isabella thought as she stared at Avery. Still, she had to tell him what he was up against. "Avery, it is only fair that you know . . ."

"No, Isabella, you don't need to say anything. I know there were rumors about something between you and Gresham at the house party." When she made to interrupt, Avery held up a stalling hand. "I must confess that those rumors are what prompted me to press you for an answer tonight. I want to announce our betrothal as a means of silencing any remnants of that gossip, for I believe that is all it is—malicious gossip from people who don't appreciate the long-standing friendship Gresham has had with your family. However, I will not condone Gresham's actions and I feel compelled to say that no gentleman would ever place a lady in such questionable circumstances. His actions were unconscionable and he should have known better."

Isabella averted her glance and looked out over the dark gardens. Avery had been doing well with his pretty speech about covering her in his honor until he'd chosen to castigate Tristan. "It's hardly fair to upbraid him when he's not here to defend himself," she found herself saying to her surprise. She'd thought she was done with standing up for Tristan.

Avery looked chastised. "My apologies. He is a particular friend of your brother's. You are absolutely correct. I should address my remarks directly to him."

Isabella smiled weakly in acceptance of his apology. She drew a deep breath and in her next response, set her life on a new course. "You have been kindness itself to me and have always treated me with the utmost respect. I accept your proposal."

Stunned, Avery could say nothing for a few joyous moments. Isabella watched rapture play across his features. Fleetingly, she let herself be caught up in his happiness. If he only knew what he was getting, she thought, coming back to earth. He might not be so jubilant. But she promised herself she'd do her best.

"I think I am the happiest man alive at this moment," Avery said at last. "I'll have our good news announced before the supper waltz."

Now that the deed was done, Isabella wanted the supper waltz to hurry as if making the announcement public would offer no opportunity to back out of it. She and Avery quietly spoke with Alain, sharing the news with him in a private room. Alain was pleasant but obviously surprised by the decision. He smiled and did his duty, saying only, "if you're sure this is what you want, Bella."

She nearly avoided having to see Tristan, but a sharp turn at the end of the ballroom during the supper waltz brought she and Avery up on the heels of Tristan and Caroline. For an instant her eyes locked with Tristan's questing gaze. She tore her gaze away. She would have no more of his treachery. How conceited he was to think he could turn his soulful gaze on her and she'd run to his arms.

She steeled herself. She would have to get used to such encounters. No doubt she and Avery would encounter Tristan and Caroline out in society and possibly even in the country on occasion with Caroline's family living so close to Avery's new horse farm. "I should warn Caroline," Isabella murmured more to herself than Avery, who looked at her quizzically and cocked his head as if he'd missed something in the conversation. When he inquired, Isabella only shook her head. Then the music was over and his Aunt Elizabeth was calling for attention. Isabella's hand tightened on Avery's arm. These next few minutes would seal her future.

Avery squeezed her hand and then left her to mount the orchestra dais and stand with his aunt. Isabella would join them after the pronouncement. It was simply done in Avery's honest, straightforward manner and soon he was gesturing for her to come up and join him as applause broke out in the ballroom. Avery was well liked by his peers and there was genuine pleasure for him as Isabella stepped onto the dais and looked out over the assembly. Many had known of his open affection for her and were pleased that his pursuit had ended successfully after his long campaign.

Of their own accord, Isabella's eyes scanned the crowd for Tristan, finding him with Caroline's family. He was all polite smiles as he bent to catch Caroline's words but he did raise his gaze to the platform once to meet her stare. Then he gave a slight conceding nod and turned his attention back to the conversation.

After supper, the evening became a blur of kisses and congratulations as well-wishers converged on them. The most horrific point of the evening occurred when Caroline pressed forward to meet them, gushing her joy. "Lady Westbrooke, you are full of surprises! I can't believe you didn't say anything to me earlier tonight." Caroline teased as she kissed Isabella's cheek. *I hadn't quite made up my mind when I saw you*, Isabella thought to herself as her ears caught the sounds of familiar low tones conversing with Avery. Her fiancé was saying, "As an old friend of the family, I hope you'll be at the wedding."

With a conspiratorial look in her direction, Tristan smiled and said, "I will be on my honeymoon in June. I am planning on taking my bride to my hunting lodge in Scotland. She's never been that far north and I want her to see the highland heather in the summer when it's at its loveliest." Avery nodded his understanding with manly consent but Isabella studied Tristan carefully. Whoever thought Tristan was doing well, didn't know him at all. How could Alain, his best friend, have thought he was fine?

He lacked his usual vitality, his voice was less animated, his bearing less alert, if that was the right word for the magnetic power that rolled off of him. When he looked at her, she knew with a certainty that she was right. His dark eyes were flat, lifeless orbs and dark circles were smudged beneath them like careless soot. Of course, the Season could take its toll with late nights and he'd put in his share of them.

But to Isabella, his hurt was obvious, if only because the façade etched on his face so closely mirrored the one she crafted for herself this evening. If anyone looked beneath the layers of cosmetics she'd used tonight to hide her own pain, they'd see much the same. Her heart lurched in a moment of weakness, forgetting that not only had she forbidden herself to feel for him, but that she was eternally furious with him for his fickle betrayal. Her mind's warning was too late. Instinctively, Isabella reached out a hand and said softly, "Tristan, are you well?"

Her tone surprised all three of them and she drew her hand back quickly once she realized what she had done, but Tristan captured it, taking her gloved hand and kissing it. Silently she acknowledged to herself why she had refused to see him. She couldn't quite bring herself to hate him and how badly she wanted to hate him!

"I am as well as can be expected, Lady Westbrooke," Tristan replied, relinquishing her hand and turning back to Avery. "Might I steal your betrothed for a dance?"

Avery graciously inclined his head while Isabella fumed. What gall these two men had to decide whom she would dance with. How neatly Tristan had maneuvered the request! Avery could not refuse and she could not contradict Avery's wishes in such a public forum. Her eyes narrowed at Tristan, the dislike for him that she failed to convincingly conjure a few moments ago, now blazed through her. With a vicious snap, she flipped open the fan that dangled from her wrist. "That was an exceedingly low move, Gresham," she said coldly as he moved them through the throng to the dance floor.

Tristan only nodded, his hand pressing on her back as he guided her on to the floor. "We aren't really going to dance, at least not past those doors on the left." There was a commanding element in his voice and his grip tightened as he swung her into the pattern. "Then we are going to find a nice quiet room where we can be alone. There are things I must say and you must hear."

"You are an arrogant man to think you can order me about like this."

"You left me no choice by refusing to see me in the privacy of your own home," Tristan retorted hotly.

The doors loomed and Tristan skillfully whirled them through the dark portals into a dimly lit hallway lined with doors. At the end of the hall he found a door ajar and the room empty. He shut the door behind them with an ominous thud that Isabella was certain the entire household heard. Her protest was cut off by a swift gesture from Tristan. "No, none of your wit will save you now, Isabella." He strode forward purposefully and grasped her by the shoulders. "I will have the truth from you, this night. You have barred me from your home, but I do not think you've so easily barred me from your heart. What game do you play with this betrothal to Driscoll?"

Isabella was outraged. "What game do I play? You are the one who used me in a misguided attempt to have my brother arrested for treason!"

"It wasn't like that. You would know the whole of it if you'd received me."

"Why should I receive you and give you another chance to worm your way back into my good graces? You've proven to be all your reputation suggested and more, a first rate blackguard." Isabella all but spat the words at him.

Tristan shook his head. "You are hurting."

"I am hating," Isabella said vehemently.

Her words struck true. Tristan released her as if scorched. He had brought her here to have a chance to explain it all to her, how the simple mission became complicated by its accidental entanglement in other innocent affairs, but her angry words fired his blood. More now than proving his blamelessness, he wanted to prove his worthiness to her, wanted her to admit that she felt nothing for Avery Driscoll. Thinking only with his ire at full throttle and not his logic, Tristan went to her again and, taking her by complete surprise, swept her into his embrace, capturing her lips in a forceful kiss that was at once both impassioned and angry in its intensity.

Isabella thought to resist. She moved her hands to his shoulders, thinking to shove him away but her traitorous body chose another course. And why not? This would be the last time those lips would seek out hers. Matrimony would keep her safe from his advances. Poppycock! Hadn't she learned that a man like Tristan stopped at nothing? No, she needed to refine that thought. There were no other men like Tristan. Tristan stopped at nothing to attain his goals. A slim band of gold would be an inconsequential obstacle to him.

All this crashed through her mind in a kaleidoscope of confusion as Tristan's lips sought hers, his tongue possessing her mouth with nimble, tantalizing movements that drove all coherent thought from her mind until she was numb with the wanting of him one last time. Isabella stumbled and lost her balance as Tristan released her. She had not expected to be released. Indeed, she'd fully expected Tristan to find some conceivable way to consummate this explosive interlude. She caught herself on the arm of the sofa and looked up at Tristan for an explanation.

His handsome face was a mottled collection of emotions from the passion that kindled his dark eyes to angry ardor that colored his firm jaw. "How can you deny this, Isabella?" he said, referring to the kiss that had passed between them. "How can you contemplate marriage to Driscoll when you know I burn for you?"

"Then, that is your misfortune," Isabella uttered the difficult words as she steeled her will to resist his next onslaught, tamping down the part of her that wished he would not take no for an answer and press her again for capitulation.

"Will you not give me a chance?" Tristan asked in a quiet, stern voice.

Isabella gave a slight negation of her head, picked up the folds of her skirt and with her head held high, walked passed him towards the door. Tristan's voice sounded behind her in a mocking tone she would not understand fully until the morning. "Then I guess there is nothing else to say but congratulations."

* * *

Betty shook Isabella awake the next morning with a jumbled message. A horse had been delivered to her stable in town and was nearly kicking out the walls of his stall. Isabella looked at her maid dazedly until Betty fumbled in her apron pocket and produced a short, curt note.

You have won him.

—Tristan.

The import of Hellion in her town stables washed over her in a wave of desolation. The ghosts of the past were no nearer to resting than they were when Tristan had first returned. Perhaps they'd never be retired. Better to live with ghosts of the past than to live with the real fear daily of being betrayed, Isabella reasoned in an attempt to quell the hurt rising in her heart. She knew how combustible the reality was of loving Tristan, how consuming it would be to live with him every day and how devastating the perfidy of his affections. Far better to live with the lesson learned instead of repeating it over and over for the duration of her life even if it meant denying the heady passion that roared between them. If not for the passion, all that lay between she and Tristan was a history of double crosses and broken hearts. They were both better off without each other. She had scorned him last night for his own good as well as her own.

Not entirely convinced of her logic, Isabella threw off the covers and rang for Betty to return to the chamber. Avery's Aunt Elizabeth was calling that afternoon to discuss wedding plans for her favorite nephew and Isabella had errands to run at the shops this morning. If she hurried she would have time to stop by the stables and check on Hellion.

Alain caught up to her at the stables, where she alone was having success in soothing Hellion in his new home. Alain grimaced upon seeing the horse. He waved to Isabella, gesturing for her to join him in the tack room.

"Alain, what are you doing here?" Isabella said, wiping her hands on a towel and retrieving her shawl from where she'd tossed it over a saddle.

"I have news you need to hear. Let's go somewhere private," Alain said somberly as he motioned towards the tack room.

"Well, what is it? Nothing bad I hope?" Isabella asked once they were alone.

"I think it depends on how one might see the situation," Alain prevaricated. "I just came from White's where I met Tristan for an eleven o'clock breakfast. He informed me that Caroline wants you to stand up with her at the wedding since I am standing up with him.

"Say something, Bella," Alain coaxed.

"Caroline mentioned the news to me last night, in confidence of course. I was not at leisure to share the news. I hope the Danvers know what they're doing by giving their daughter to him," she said at last.

Alain gave a snort. "They're in alt. Caroline has snared a significant title and fortune with nothing to recommend her to such a peer but her good looks, pleasant demeanor and social connections through you," he paused, his gaze suddenly interested in something beyond her left shoulder. "I hope you understand I am not picking sides in this whole travesty, but if his best friend doesn't stand up with him at his wedding who will? And of course I can hardly refuse when I have it on good authority that Caroline will ask you to be her matron of honor."

His last words shocked her and Isabella had to put out a hand to steady herself. It would be the final test of her resolve to put Tristan out of her life to stand mere feet away from Tristan on his wedding day. The convoluted workings of her numb brain wondered if Tristan hadn't put Caroline up to it out of some need to punish her for rejecting him. What could she say to refuse Caroline? Nothing wouldn't raise speculation. She had to accept.

Along with being Avery Driscoll's June bride, Isabella found herself a bridesmaid to Caroline Danvers. The ensuing two weeks were tortuous beyond anything Torquemada could have devised. Caroline consulted her endlessly on the details of her rushed wedding to Tristan. The young bride developed an annoying habit of inserting into conversation regularly how romantic it was that Tristan wanted to whisk her off to Scotland to see the heather at its finest and to have her to himself. Additionally, each day presented its own special form of agony as Isabella's nerves stayed on edge with the worry that she might encounter Tristan. Only once did the worry manifest itself.

Tristan called at the Danvers' home one afternoon while Isabella was assisting Caroline with the selection of household linen. She'd frozen the minute she'd caught his voice in the hall. Caroline had looked up from her pile of swatches, beaming as she recognized the voice, too. She rose and went to the door of the little parlor calling, "Darling, we're in here. Come and see the linen samples."

Isabella winced at the summons. She'd hoped Caroline might go into the hall and converse with Tristan there instead of dragging him into the room and into her presence. Within seconds of the summons, boots sounded on the tile in the hall outside the parlor and Tristan materialized in the doorway, stopping to place a dutiful kiss on Caroline's cheek. Isabella didn't avert her gaze fast enough. Tristan looked beyond Caroline's shoulder and saw her staring at them. She was gratified to see the tic in his cheek jump at the sight of her as he strode toward the sofa where she sat. He inclined his head and was all appropriate formality.

"Lady Westbrooke, it is so kind of you to spare your time for Caroline when I know you have the pressing matter of your own wedding to consider as well."

Caroline gushed from his side, looking ever more dolllike in the shadow of Tristan's dominating presence. "Yes, you are a dear to do this for me. I don't know how Mother and I would have gotten everything ready in just two weeks."

"Our families have been friends and neighbors for a long time, Caroline. It is an honor that you've asked me," Isabella managed to reply before turning her attention back to the linen swatches in the vain hope that Caroline and Tristan would leave her alone. She hadn't an ounce of luck.

"Oh yes, come and see what we've picked out. Lady Westbrooke has helped me narrow the samples down to just five for our formal linen." Caroline drew Tristan forward to the little table in front of the sofa, indicating the five patterns. She pointed at one pattern specifically. "I prefer the embossed roses for the table linen."

Tristan reached out a hand and covered Caroline's gently, his fingers offering a soft caress as he did so. "I don't think I'd prefer the roses, Caro."

Caroline turned her big blue eyes up to him, all acquiescence. "Of course, darling. Perhaps the white damask then?"

He nodded his approval and Isabella bristled while he caressed Caroline's hand again in an obvious manner, the affects of the tender gesture blatant on Caroline's face as she suppressed a giggle. "You're so naughty, my lord," she chided.

Good lord, if you think that's naughty, wait until he sticks his tongue in your mouth, Isabella thought uncharitably as Tristan took leave of his blushing bride. The next time she saw Tristan was two weeks later at the wedding.

Chapter Fourteen

Despite the hurried nature of the affair, the stone church dating back to Norman times on the Danvers' property was filled to capacity with well-wishers the morning of the wedding. Even the mercurial weather had decided to cooperate, giving the bride a blue-skied day to remember her nuptials. Caroline was resplendent in a white satin gown, heavily encrusted with pearls. If the bride was lovely, the groom was a breathtaking vision of manliness.

Tristan stood straight and pale at the altar, attired most excellently in a dark blue morning frock coat of Bath superfine and ivory inexpressibles, a pristine cravat tied in an elegant "oriental" at his throat with a diamond pin winking tastefully in its folds. His dark hair was pulled back in a perfectly executed queue, setting off the firm lines of his face. His straight shoulders never slouched, the alert pose of his body showing nothing beyond the typical tension of a bridegroom. If he was aware of the ladies that commented slyly on his good looks and rakish reputation behind their hands in the pews, his actions made no note of it. In fact, anyone standing close to him could see the flatness in his usually vibrant eyes and sense the void that was regularly filled with his vital energy.

Alain stood rigidly at attention next to Tristan, his mossy

eyes intent on the scene unfolding before him. The entire morning, since the minute he had awakened had seemed surreal to him. An indefinable sixth sense warned him about the day. It was not enough that his friend was marrying the wrong woman. Something more was wrong, very wrong, about the occasion. But despite his misgivings, the incredible, terrible day had unfolded without incident. He'd managed to get both he and Tristan suitably attired and off to the church without mishap. He'd even attempted an awkward conversation with Tristan in a last attempt to guide him away from this ill-conceived marriage. His efforts had been useless. Here they were, dutifully waiting for the bride and enduring the scrutiny of the guests as they stood at the front of the be-garlanded church.

The guests stilled suddenly and heads swiveled as Isabella glided down the aisle dressed in pale blue satin and lace, her arrival heralding that the bride was at hand. Alain watched his friend's jaw clench and his fists tighten at his sides. Alain noted how Tristan's eyes followed Isabella up to the altar where she took her place on the left side of the aisle. Even after the crowd aahed at the first sighting of the bride in the church doorway, Tristan's eyes struggled to leave Isabella.

Isabella fought the temptation to look slightly to the right in fear of catching Tristan's eye. Determinedly, she looked straight out into the pews, trying to lose herself in the sea of faces that swam before her, but nothing could shake her consciousness of Tristan's probing stare. She knew she was pale. She'd seen her face in the mirror that morning while Betty conducted her toilette. She was utterly unaware that her paleness simply served to enhance her ethereal beauty against the folds of her pale blue bridesmaid's dress.

A voice in her head that would not be silenced by any device she had yet created dared her to put a stop to the ceremony, to cross the six feet that separated her from Tristan and confess her soul to him; that she had wrestled the night away with her conscience and found in the dawn the ultimate truth of her heart; she was only marrying Avery because she was too frightened to marry Tristan, too frightened of the betrayals she might face. If he gave her just one word of encouragement, she would be his. The voice in her head begged her to ask Tristan for those words now as the last minutes of opportunity ticked away. She resisted. If she could last the hour, there would be no more temptation. In all ways that mattered, Tristan would be dead to her. She fought her demons, she would not look at him.

She would not look at him! Tristan's heart plunged further. This was not his wedding, but his funeral, Tristan thought as he gazed on the pageantry of the event unfolding before him with eyes that saw the irony of it all. The occasion was not so much a ceremony of joining, but a ceremony of separation; not so much the beginning of new life but the ending of an old one. Indeed, he was already dead in the ways that had come to matter to him. Everything down to his very clothing symbolized a departure from his former self. He was not marrying in his military dress uniform. That avenue of his life was closed to him now, too. His career and his true love, were both part of his past. Neither was part of his future.

He was vaguely aware from the stir among the guests that Caroline had entered the church. Duty required he look at her with the gaze of an expectant and well-pleased bridegroom but the bride of his heart stood just a few feet away. He found his stare defiantly fixed on Isabella's pale face, his memory taking in the whole of her as she did her best to hide her trembling hands beneath the abundant bouquet she carried. What would she do if he risked all and stepped across the dais, swept her into his arms and carried her out of the church? His coach was waiting outside. They'd be in Scotland within days and they'd never have to come home. In fact, after such action, there could be no other choice.

When he could no longer bear her countenance, Tristan tore his eyes from her and watched Caroline Danvers come down the aisle, the epitome of the perfect, golden-haired bride, and take her place next to him.

The reverend intoned the opening words of the ceremony. Tristan's eyes fell on the worn Bible in his hands.

Halfway through the ceremony, Tristan's dazed attention focused on a growing tension beside him. Alain stirred infinitesimally by his side. Tristan attributed his movement as a signal that it was time for the ring. Alain handed him the ring and Tristan noted his friend had taken the opportunity to readjust himself so that he could now see past Isabella on the left side and out into the front rows of guests. Alert now, Tristan divided his attention. With only half of his concentration, Tristan listened to Caroline recite her pledge to him while he held the ring in readiness for the giving of his own vows. The other portion of his focus was on Isabella.

Isabella stilled as she felt Tristan's gaze on her. Her first, fleeting thought was that Tristan was going to embarrass her with some last minute foolishness, then she realized he wasn't looking at her but beyond her to someone else.

"Gresham!" An angry voice rang out behind her as stifled screams emitted from the audience. Alain surged forward, tackling Caroline to the floor and covering her with his protective form. Isabella pivoted to find the voice, having only a moment to take in the sight of Middleton with a deadly pistol raised in her direction. It vaguely crossed her mind that the shot was not meant for her but that she was in the bullet's path, a thought Middleton hadn't had time to process before he pulled the trigger, firing the shot meant for Tristan.

"Bella!" Tristan roared, using his whole body to roughly shove her aside, her scream swallowed in the wake of his own shout. She stumbled, falling away from him as everything in her world slowed. With horrified eyes she watched Tristan's body ingest the full impact of the bullet striking his chest. He gave a cry as he hit the floor and went still.

"Tristan!" Isabella scrambled across the floor to his side, her skirt ripping as it tangled with her knees as she crawled to him, barely aware of Alain launching himself from the dais onto Middleton and wrestling him to the ground. Someone rushed forward to Caroline who appeared to have fainted. She heard Giles directing people out of the church and away from the mess at the altar. In the ensuing chaos, it was Chatham and Avery who found their way to her side and helped her to tear back the fabric of Tristan's clothing and ascertain the extent of the wound.

"Tear up your underskirts," Chatham commanded urgently. "We've got to stop the bleeding if it's possible."

"Possible? What do you mean?" Panic edged her voice as her trembling hands began ripping as Chatham ordered.

"The bullet may have hit an artery. There's so much blood, too much blood," Chatham said, his hands probing the wound for further clarification. "Now, tear me long strips of cloth. If we can staunch the bleeding, we can bind the wound long enough to get him to the house."

Avery took one look at Isabella's stricken face and galvanized into action. "I'll go for the doctor and have him meet us at the manor house."

Isabella thought the waiting would drive her insane as she paced the Danvers' parlor. The room was crowded with Tristan's friends. Giles and Chatham sat, legs outstretched, untouched snifters of brandy in their hands. Alain stared out the window in the oncoming twilight. Avery stood stoically by the door. In a corner on the sofa, Caroline cried intermittently into a handkerchief, her radiant face blotchy, her gown crushed and wrinkled.

Several events had transpired while Tristan lay unconscious in the hands of the surgeon. Alain had brought down Middleton and the local officials had taken him into town to be held until the appropriate magistrates could pick him up for questioning. Giles, after organizing the evacuation of the church and seeing to the guests, had the unwelcome task of explaining to Caroline that her almost-husband was a secret agent for the crown.

Avery had said nothing after summoning the doctor but had stood silently watching them all as they waited for the surgeon's verdict. He was acutely aware that he was an outsider to these affairs, as was Caroline, regardless of the fact that it was her house. The two of them were not part of this tight knit group that waited anxiously for news of their dear friend. He had no doubt that Caroline would not complete her wedding to Gresham. Just as he knew with a dread certainty that he would not see his marriage to Isabella come to fruition in June. He didn't belong here but he stayed for Isabella. If the worst should happen, she would need what comfort he could offer and he would give it freely. A movement in the room caught his eye. His gaze shifted, following Caroline as she crossed the room to Isabella and touched her gently on the sleeve.

Isabella felt a lite touch on her arm and heard Caroline whisper beside her. "Come walk with me."

The two women strolled the hallway, coming to stop by a window that overlooked the back gardens. At length, Caroline spoke. "I must speak frankly with you, Lady Westbrooke. This has been a nightmarish day, this wedding that wasn't. We weren't truly married, you know. He never spoke his vows." There was a break in her voice as it trembled. "And he never will, at least he will never speak them to me."

At a loss, Isabella struggled to find comforting words. "He will recover. He is a strong man. The wedding can take place later."

"No. I cannot marry him now that I know," Caroline sniffed. "I cannot live with the danger that surrounds him. I am not naive enough to believe that his enemies will leave him alone, that there will be no repeats of attacks like the one today. I haven't your courage, Lady Westbrooke. Even more so, I cannot marry a man who loves another. I saw it in his eyes today that he loves you. When I came down the aisle, every pair of eyes were on me, but not his. He was looking at you as if you were his life and when he did look at me, his eyes were dead. I do not want to live with a shell of a man, knowing that his very sorrow stems from being with me."

"I don't know what to say," Isabella stammered. "I think perhaps you overrate the situation," she offered the hasty denial, thinking to spare Caroline's feelings. No bride should discover on her wedding day that the groom favored the bridesmaid.

"Don't pretend it isn't true," Caroline said with a quiet sternness that did her credit. "He took that bullet for you. Middleton realized too late that you were in the line of fire. Whatever doubts you had about Tristan's devotion to you, you can doubt no longer." Tears threatened to overcome her after her brave speech. "I will retire privately for a few moments, if you'll excuse me?" Caroline turned and fled to an empty room, overwhelmed.

Isabella walked slowly back to the parlor alone. Caroline's words confirmed the truths she had recognized as she'd knelt next to Tristan on the dais. She and Tristan belonged together but that knowledge had come too late. She'd seen the wound first hand when Chatham had pulled the blood soaked cloth of Tristan's shirt away from his chest. She had seen the futility of the white wadding Chatham had pressed against the gaping hole as pad after pad of her underskirt had become drenched in Tristan's blood. That Chatham had been able to get Tristan stabilized enough to get to the manor house a half mile away had been nothing short of miraculous. She did not think she'd get another miracle.

The surgeon confirmed her worst suspicions when she returned to the parlor. Tristan would not last the night. The bullet had been removed and had impossibly missed striking his heart or lungs, but the extraction and the loss of blood had weakened him considerably. Already, he was in the throes of a fever with no strength left to fight it.

"It's only a fever! Surely you can do something for him? Give him something to help him fight!" Isabella lashed out angrily at the doctor, who spread his hands helplessly against her tirade. "You can't let him simply slip away! You can't give up." Her eyes were wild in her desperation.

It was Avery who stepped in when the others were silent, ingesting their own desperation over Tristan. "Of course, we won't let him give up." He had tried for two years to make Isabella happy. He saw clearly now why he'd fallen short of the mark. Her heart had never been hers to give, for it had been given years ago. Her happiness would be his parting gift to her. He would fight with her for Tristan's life. He felt Alain step up beside him, having recovered himself sufficiently to see his sister's incredible need. "We will fight for him, Bella, just as he has fought for us."

The group drew watches and set their guard around their friend, bathing him as his fever raged; pressing a glass of water between his lips to assuage his thirst, checking his bandages to ensure bleeding hadn't begun again. Avery took Isabella aside and forced her to rest, saying that if Tristan were to die it would be at the bridge of the night as dark passed to dawn. He would need her then to fight the ebbing tides that would tug at his soul and lure him away as surely as any siren of mythology lured Odysseus. True to his word, Avery fetched her for the fourth watch.

Isabella was not ready for the sight that lay before her as she entered the sickroom. Tristan was a pale, lifeless form in the midst of the big bed, only his dark hair contrasted with the white linens around him. She thought for a moment that he'd already slipped away without waking. Alain sat by the bed, his head drooping in weariness.

"Alain?" Her voice quaked with her unspoken fear. She looked to her brother for hope.

Alain had none to give her as he rose from the chair near the bed, his face stubbled, and his voice hoarse as he spoke. "He is struggling, Bella. You can see how shallow his breathing is." He nodded at the covers, which barely rose beneath Tristan's chest.

"The fever has him quite thoroughly now. He tried to leave a few hours ago, I think, but I took his hand and began to talk to him of our days at school together and all the funny pranks I could remember. It seemed to help." Alain paused, unsure what more to say.

"What is it?" Isabella said, reading the indecision on her brother's face.

"I think I called him back because he waits for you," Alain said softly. "If you can find him in the fever, I think you alone could bring him back. Give him something to fight with, Bella."

When Alain left, she took up her vigil on the side of the big bed, eschewing the chair for Tristan's side. She took his limp hand in her own, amazed at how hot his skin burned. It was almost uncomfortable to hold on to him, but she did not flinch. She began to talk of their summers at Summer Hill, of the river and the horses and the picnics. She imagined his brow relaxed and became peaceful as the stories of their picnics and river walks wove their magic around him. Unmistakably, she felt the hand in her own grow increasingly slack and anger welled up inside her. He would not cheat her again!

"Tristan! Wake up. I did not give you permission to leave." She raised her voice. "You will not break my heart a third time. I will not allow it. I love you and I will not give you up to this. Come back and give us a chance, Tristan. Don't leave me, Tristan!"

She cupped his face between her hands and put her face close to his and began reciting the first thing that came to mind. "I take thee, Tristan Alexander Moreland, fourth Viscount Gresham, to be my lawfully wedded husband, to have and hold in sickness and in health, for richer for poorer, until death do us part." She sobbed openly as the words tumbled out in disorder, begging and pledging all at once as she repeated her litany in anger, in desperation.

* * *

He was dying and it was lovely, Tristan thought as he floated through peaceful memories. At first it had been very painful. Middleton's bullet had wrought a terrible amount of damage when it struck him. He had fallen, finding in the chaos Isabella's piercing, healthy screams. She was safe. Then the burning in his chest had claimed all of his attention as he struggled for consciousness. Chatham was there, tearing at his clothes and Isabella was there, far more terrified than he'd ever seen her, which had to be a good sign. At the end, she loved him at least a little and that was something. After the pain, there had been peace. He heard Alain's voice calling to him and the five of them were all together at the estate at the lakes, running and riding and laughing. They were younger and happy. They were picnicking and Isabella had made him a crown of daisies to wear on his head while the others laughed affectionately.

Ah, God had been good to him after all, to give him this paradise for all eternity, the one place where he'd felt at home, the one time in his life when his soul hadn't been so dark, with the people he'd loved most in his life. Isabella was laughing up at him now, her topaz eyes alight with the joy of being with him as they walked down by the river, the other boys off in the distance.

Up ahead the boys were calling to him to join them. He would go to them and stay in this blessed place forever, but Isabella would not let go of his arm. He tugged gently but her hold tightened and she was pleading with him, mouthing words he could not understand at first. Realization dawned. They were the words of the marriage ceremony and she was repeating them over and over as she begged him to stay.

He resisted her, his desire to go with the boys growing. In exasperation, he pulled once more and he felt all her strength go into her arms as she held onto him. He heard the words her mouth formed, "I love you. Do not leave me." At last, he relented. A sense of happiness flooded him now that he'd made his decision to stay. But the boys had run up to him, and were tugging now at him, forcing him to join them in their play. He cried out to Isabella, "Don't let them have me. I will stay." He felt her lend him the strength he'd fought against moments ago. A new sense of power infused him and Tristan felt the boys fall back vanquished. Isabella gathered him into her arms murmuring a litany of words he could not make out. Then his paradise disappeared and there was nothing but darkness and peace.

"There is much to hope for if he has lasted the night," the surgeon declared to Tristan's friends the next morning after checking on the patient. "His fever is diminished. He is breathing deeply and his wound has not bled. He is not safe yet, but we may hope."

His friends kept their vigil three more days, each day bringing with it renewed hope that Tristan would survive the ordeal. On the fourth day, he awoke to find Isabella sitting next to him. She jumped in surprise as his eyes opened. "I'll get the others," she cried, rising from her chair. Tristan gave a weak shake of his head and said one hoarse word, "sit."

Isabella sat and lifted a glass of water to his lips. His voice was stronger after the drink. "Are you well?" he asked, his brown eyes searching her tired face. "Do you love me? Do you still wish to marry me?"

"Yes. You heard me?" Isabella's eyes filled with tears as she was overcome by emotion. She grasped his hand and knelt by the bed. "You nearly left us. Oh, Tristan, I couldn't bear you dying. I didn't know what else to do. I've been so foolish about loving you."

"We've both been foolish," Tristan said, reveling in the feel of her hand around his own. "At the wedding, I wondered what would happen if I crossed the dais, carried you out to my coach and simply drove off. I was so close to doing just that. What would you have done, Isabella?"

"Need you ask?" Isabella said. "I am beyond caring about scandal and reputations. I would have gone with you. I was wondering much the same thing. I wanted to cross the dais and confess the truth to you, that I loved you."

Tristan smiled weakly and turned somber. "How is Caroline? And the others?"

"Everyone is doing well. Caroline's parents have packed her off to London. The events of the wedding have been portrayed quite sympathetically. She'll be little harmed by the gossip, I think. If anything, it will increase her cache this Season. We've all stayed on to look after you, even Avery. He's ridden over daily from his stables to help." She added for clarification, "he knows that our engagement is null." She and Avery had not discussed it, but one night she'd simply taken the engagement sapphire off her finger and slipped it wordlessly into his palm. He had looked at her, tight-lipped and drawn and nodded in acceptance.

"Then there are no impediments to our marriage?" Tristan asked.

"No."

"I wish us to marry as soon as possible."

Framed by the rays of a sunny mid-May morning, Isabella stood in the archway of the stone church at Summer Hill, savoring the scent of spring wild flowers mixed with the best roses Tristan's greenhouses had to offer. Vicar Hurley looked regal in his black robes at the front of the little church. Beside him, Tristan stood rigidly, the white of his sling stark against the dark blue of his morning coat. He was otherwise impeccably turned out. His face was slightly pale from the journey to Summer Hill. She had tried to counsel rest and patience but Tristan had been adamant that they wait no longer to begin their life together.

The three musicians they'd hired from the village began to play a soft country tune. Tears welled in Isabella's eyes. This was the wedding she'd always dreamed of: the friendly old vicar presiding over a small service among her friends as she pledged herself to the man she loved. She cast a quick look down at the unpretentious rose muslin gown she wore, adorned with the simplest of gros grain ribbon trim and Nottingham lace at the neck. The gown was much different than the one she'd worn when she wedded Westbrooke. She was much different.

Alain appeared at her side to usher her down the aisle before taking his place next to Tristan. "Tristan is holding up well. Don't let his paleness alarm you. I think it's just bridegroom nerves," he whispered. "Are you ready?"

Isabella could only nod.

She shed tears as Tristan spoke his vows to her and slipped the simple gold band on her finger. Her hands shook as she put her own ring on Tristan's scarred hand. Tristan covered her hands with his own until the shaking abated. In no time, the ceremony was complete. The vicar pronounced them man and wife. Tristan bent to kiss her, a honest offering of his love.

Isabella smiled up at him as they walked down the aisle. They stole a moment for themselves in the church anteroom before going out into the sunlight and the throngs of villagers who awaited them.

"It is done, at last. You're mine, for always," Tristan said reverently, helping her drape a light rose patterned shawl about her shoulders.

"I never dreamed I'd win so much when I wagered with Alain," Isabella beamed.

"To win much, much must be risked," Tristan pointed out sagely.

"I agree with that! I thought I was only pitting my matchmaking skills against a silly fortune. It took me awhile to realize I had wagered my heart," Isabella admitted shyly. She pressed close to Tristan and gazed up at him, a mischievous smile playing about her lips. "I am glad you married me, Tristan, only you can save me now."

Tristan started to laugh as he recalled her words from

years ago. "It is only fitting that our story ends as it began, isn't it, Bella?"

"You're wrong, Tristan. This is not the end," Isabella said softly, rising slightly on her toes to plant a promising kiss on his lips.

Chapter Fifteen

The Meadows, February 14, 1817

"Salud!" glasses clinked as the five friends gathered around the fireplace where roaring fire crackled in the hearth. It was only seven o'clock in the evening. Valentine's evening was still young by London standards. There would be time to toast the day of love later. This toast was for the new one in their midst. "Our circle has grown larger by one. To little Alain Alexander!" Giles led them in his toast. They all raised their glasses in tribute to the month old infant that snuggled contently in Isabella's arms.

Tristan reached out a finger for the baby to grab and smiled at Isabella, his whole heart etched on his face as he did so. He was a man well contented. This Valentine's Day he had so much to celebrate. Isabella was his wife, at last. The Meadows was thriving under his direction and Isabella's dedication. His stables blossomed with two promising new foals sired by Hellion. In the fall, Isabella's pregnancy provided a brilliant excuse to forego the little Season in London. They spent Christmas and New Year's surrounded by their friends at The Meadows as they anticipated the arrival of their child. Alain Alexander made his appearance early, January tenth.

If he never set foot in London again, he'd be content. All he truly needed in life was here at The Meadows.

The nurse came to take the sleeping baby and Tristan reluctantly gave up his son's hand as Isabella turned her wide eyes in his direction, full of an overwhelming love for him. She wore a magnificent gown in deep carnelian velvet that reminded him of both fire and the sun, the two images he most closely associated with her. He bent to kiss her hand while Giles called for attention.

"Everyone, for our Valentine's Day together, I've planned something special," he began as the others laughed.

"No, not after last year!" Chatham pleaded good-naturedly. "Look where your antics landed poor Tristan!"

Giles made a great show of puzzling over the thought and then said in mockingly playful tones, "Ah yes, Tristan ended up married to his best friend's lovely sister. Poor Tristan indeed! We should all wish ourselves to be so lucky!"

"You could not be luckier than I," Tristan said with great humor. He lifted his glass to salute himself. "It's Isabella who must have your pity. All she got out of the deal was a wild stallion." The group laughed.

Isabella rose and placed her hands saucily on her hips and tossed her head. "I beg your pardon, I got *two* wild stallions and I tamed them both." She reached up and put her arms around Tristan's neck, drawing him close for a kiss that held the promise of more while the others clinked their glasses and roared their approval.